"...A joy to read!" — Ken Bruen
(author of the *Jack Taylor* series)

PAROLE

"...A tale that is hard to put down and
satisfyingly original: a standout in its genre." —
Diane Donovan, *Midwest Book Review*

Also by Bruce Hartman:

PAROLE

a novel

Bruce Hartman

Swallow Tail Press

PAROLE

Published by Swallow Tail Press
Philadelphia, PA, USA
www.swallowtailpress.com
Also available in ebook format

ISBN: 9780999756430

1

The driver's window of the black BMW glided open and a .45-caliber Glock settled into firing position. Under a foggy street light in downtown L.A., a man stepped off the Bolt Bus lugging a plastic garbage bag — a skinny white guy in gray sweats who looked like an aging skinhead — followed by a big black guy, also in gray sweats, a Mexican woman lugging a battered suitcase, and a little girl.

Three shots flared out from the Glock in the car window.

People shouted, screamed, howled.

More shots and the men went down, dragging the woman and the girl with them.

All of them lay motionless, silent, bleeding on the sidewalk.

The men sprawled on the sidewalk were Kenny Ruffin and Cat McGrath. They had been paroled out of San Quentin that morning and stuck on the same bus back to L.A. Inside the prison they instinctively hated each other — Ruffin was black, McGrath white — and if they'd ever made eye contact, one of them would probably have ended up dead on the laundry floor. Now, squeezed together next to the stinking toilet in the back of the bus, they were supposed to play nice.

"You ever been paroled before?" McGrath — the white guy — said out loud without looking at Ruffin. His face was wizened and blotchy, his neck ringed with tattooed snakes and American flags. The first thing you noticed about him was his new white prison teeth, a going-away present from the warden who hoped never to see him again. "Well, I been in and out a few times so I know the drill. You spend your time inside waiting for the big day when you finally get out. But believe me, outside is a helluva lot worse than inside. You think it's bad in Quentin? Maybe you forgot what things is like out here. Just as bad as inside — worse, only more complicated, more dangerous."

Would he have to listen to this peckerwood all the way to L.A.? Ruffin wondered. That eight hours was going to be like spending another ten years in the joint.

"You gotta watch your ass every minute," McGrath went on. "On the inside you know who your enemies are. Turn your back on them and you're a dead man."

Same as out here, Ruffin thought. Try it and find out.

"Outside, you can't trust nobody, especially your parole agent, unless you want to be his bitch for the time you're outside."

The time I'm outside? Ruffin bristled. What's he talking about? He thinks I'm going back inside?

"Oh, you'll go back in," McGrath said, reading his mind. "Everybody goes back in — that's how the system works. But you want to make the most of your time on the outside. The first thing I'm gonna do when we get off this bus is get laid."

"The first thing I'm gonna do," Ruffin said, "is kick your ass. The second thing is kick it again."

"That would be a parole violation," McGrath smiled, showing off his new teeth. "From now on, everything you do is gonna be a parole violation. You look cross-eyed at a cop, that's a parole violation. You don't eat your mashed potatoes, that's a parole violation. You wear the wrong color lipstick when you kiss your parole agent's ass, that's a parole violation."

"Don't you ever shut your mouth?"

"Now that you mention it, I guess I don't. Folks been telling me that all my life, even my own dear mama. 'Son,' she said, 'if you don't stop your damn babbling I'm gonna knock that pacifier down your throat.' But I just can't do it. It's a weakness, I admit. Been that way all my life."

Ruffin was a tall, muscular man with a high forehead, a pair of lively eyes and a wary, almost bashful smile. Women, back in the days when he knew any women, used to flock around him purring like kittens. His charm and good looks hadn't worked as well on the cops or the prosecutors. Facing life in prison at the age of twenty-one, he'd pled guilty to armed robbery, conspiracy to commit murder, possession of illegal drugs with intent to sell, pimping and pandering, and unlawful possession of firearms, and drew a twenty-year sentence. That's what his Legal Aid lawyer called a bargain. Looking back, he had to admit he'd been a pretty bad dude. Was he still just as bad as he was then? Was he rotten at the core, like the prosecutor said, an incorrigible career criminal like this fool sitting next to him on the bus? He didn't really know. He'd never really meant any harm, never wanted to kill anybody. So he got twenty years hard time and felt lucky to be paroled after seventeen for good behavior.

When he went inside, good behavior was the last thing he thought he'd be guilty of. At twenty-one, he was a six-foot four-inch, 250-pound prison riot waiting to happen. But as the years went by he mellowed out, took up meditation, helped some of the other prisoners deal with their issues, which, surprisingly, were a lot worse than his. He wasn't a drug addict, he didn't have HIV or Hep-C, he wasn't a violent, burned-out shell who couldn't be allowed back on the street. He had no family, no education, no job — there was plenty to be bitter about — and he didn't have any illusions about becoming a fine upstanding pillar of the community. But he had a teenage son he'd never seen — a boy named Jayden who was born after he went inside — and he was willing to do what he needed to do to keep from having to go back inside. After all he'd been through, all the lessons he'd learned, all the temptations he'd resisted, all the shit he'd had to eat — how hard could it be to stay out of jail?

At least that's what he thought until he had to spend eight hours on the bus sitting next to McGrath.

McGrath was out of Quentin after eight years of a ten-year term. Everybody was glad to see him go. Pushing fifty, full sleeve tattoos up to his chin and a smart mouth that couldn't stop flapping — everything about him cried out for a shank in the back but he never got one. The guards called him The Cat Came Back because he'd been in and out of the joint so many times. He just couldn't stay away. And nobody wanted to mess with him because if he survived, which he always did, they'd never hear the end of it. Even the Aryan Brotherhood didn't want him.

McGrath talked in a twangy country western voice that made Ruffin want to plug his ears or jump out the window, yet he droned on and on as if he thought Ruffin was hanging on every word. Ruffin considered punching him out, choking him, knocking out his new prison teeth, anything to make him shut up, but he asked himself: why should he let this pissant ruin his life? He felt hot, sweaty, pissed off like his first year in the joint. The feeling scared him.

"On the ranch where I growed up," McGrath twanged, "there was nothing to talk about and nobody to say it to. Still I never stopped to take a breath till they sent me to reform school. It was a vocational school and I found out my vocation was crime. Been at it ever since."

There was one thing, Ruffin admitted to himself, that McGrath was right about — so far, outside was a lot worse than inside. When they let you out of San Quentin, they don't give you $50 and a new suit and let you walk out the gate. They give you a pair of gray sweats like you could buy at Walmart for $12.99 and lock you in an armored van with a couple of guards carrying Smith & Wesson .38s who drive you along San Francisco Bay to a turnout on I-580 near San Quentin Point where you catch the Bolt Bus to L.A. Ruffin and McGrath were like a couple of animals locked by mistake in the same cage.

That morning the guards were a couple of good old boys named Crocker and Dixon. When they stopped at the turnout, Dixon handed Ruffin and McGrath a sheet of paper with a picture of their parole agent and his address and phone number in L.A. "Listen up, scumbags," he said. "This is Harold Chung, your parole agent. Starting today you're on parole and Harold

Chung is the god you pray to. You keep him happy, we won't be seeing you up here again. Piss him off and you'll wish you never got out. Your appointment's at 1:00 o'clock tomorrow afternoon and you damn well better show up for it." He flashed a vicious smile. "Good luck."

A bus with LOS ANGELES on the front pulled up at the curb. Dixon slipped out and climbed on the bus to chat with the driver. Crocker peered at the cons in the rearview mirror. "Your tickets to L.A. have been paid for. The driver will drop you off at the shelter."

"I ain't staying in no shelter," McGrath said.

"Ruffin's staying in the shelter," Crocker said. "So that's where you both get off."

When Dixon came back, Ruffin and McGrath climbed out of the van carrying the black plastic garbage bags that held everything they owned. They set their feet down gently, as if they were testing the ground, half expecting to sink in or be blown away by the wind. This was the first time either of them had touched the ground — the real ground, not the prison ground — in years. They didn't speak to each other. McGrath asked Dixon for a match to light a cigarette, took one puff and threw it down on the pavement. Cars and trucks hammered past them on the freeway a few feet away. Ruffin spit and followed McGrath onto the bus.

"How'd the Cat end up on the same bus as that animal?" Crocker asked Dixon, back in the van.

"Somebody in the Warden's office must have a sense of humor."

They laughed as Crocker turned the van around. "Two days ago they would have torn each other's throats out if you left them together for thirty seconds."

"Don't give up hope," Dixon said. "It's a long ride down to L.A."

As Ruffin and McGrath climbed on the bus the driver waved them toward the back. "Sit in the rear seat and don't start any trouble," he said.

They sat down next to the toilet without looking at each other. Ruffin smiled at a cute little girl in the seat in front of them and she smiled back at him. She was with her mother, who pulled her back around, muttering something in Spanish.

Ruffin stared out the window at the dry California landscape. The world he'd tried to forget about for seventeen years was flashing by so fast he could hardly see it, let alone think about it. Farms, trees, houses, office buildings, common enough things that looked so unfamiliar they might have just arrived from outer space. What were the people going to be like out here? How would he be able to deal with them?

"You can get away with anything if you don't stop talking," McGrath said. "If I'd a gone to college I could have been a lawyer or a politician. Cat McGrath, Esquire. Senator Cat McGrath. Probably have a prison named after me by now."

Ruffin stood up and opened the door to the toilet and squeezed himself inside. It smelled bad and he couldn't turn around, but that was okay, he just needed to get away from McGrath. Even in there you could hear him jangling on like he thought the world was waiting to hear what he had to say. Five minutes, ten minutes, fifteen minutes and no sign of him letting up. Then somebody banged on the door and Ruffin had to squeeze out and face the music. "Them sons of bitches in Quentin beat me up, threw me in the hole, tried to kill me nine ways from Sunday," McGrath was saying, as if Ruffin had been sitting there all along. "But they couldn't shut me up, no matter what they did."

Ruffin dropped back into his seat and looked McGrath straight in the eyes, something he hadn't done to any man in years. They weren't the furtive, hostile eyes you see in the joint — no, they glistened with the same crazed eagerness that poured out of his mouth, the self-confidence that somehow had survived eight years in San Quentin. What could you do with a man like that? You could crush him, suffocate him, hammer him into the ground. But was there any way you could just make him shut up?

"Finally," McGrath went on, "they said Cat, the judge thinks this prison's overcrowded and you ain't worth the dogshit we're feeding you, so we might as well let you go. You been punished enough. And it don't matter because the first day you're out of here somebody's gonna finish you off cause you talk too damn much."

He stared back at Ruffin to make sure he had his attention. "So they stuck me on this bus with you, Ruffin, hoping you'd be the one to do it."

Ruffin jumped up and stalked down the aisle looking for an empty seat. The driver called out, "Hey you, stay in the back or I'm gonna throw you off the bus."

He glared at the driver, at the passengers, who looked out the window, staring at their phones, pretending not to see him. Finally at the little girl — she must have been about six — who thought he was funny. He smiled at her and slid back into his seat, shoving McGrath out of the way with his elbow.

"Shut your mouth," he said.

"I told you I can't do that," McGrath said. "The question is, what are you gonna do about it? You gonna make me shut it? I doubt it. No offense, but you ain't the man you used to be. None of us is."

Ruffin grabbed McGrath's tattooed wrist and twisted it like he meant to break it. McGrath barely flinched, but he offered a kind of apology: "I wouldn't say that if we was still inside."

"If we was still inside," Ruffin said, "you'd be dead by now."

2

The bus stopped at a rest area where the passengers could buy snacks and stretch their legs. Away from the coast the sun was blazing hot, about 95 degrees, and after all those years in the joint Ruffin could hardly stand to open his eyes. McGrath paced around in the shade sucking on a cigarette, his face animated by tics and twitches as if the monologue was still going on inside his head. Ruffin went inside and spent four dollars of his gate money on a black coffee and a bag of chips. He waited inside until the bus was filling up and climbed back on just as the driver started the engine. Skinny as he was, McGrath tried to hog half of Ruffin's seat and had to be muscled aside. Ruffin offered to share his chips with the little girl, but her mother, who didn't speak English, pulled her away.

McGrath's mouth idled like the bus, gathering energy for the next leg of the journey. "It's a different world out here," he said as they glided back on the freeway. "Different from inside and different from the one you left behind. Think you're ready for it?"

Ruffin clapped his hands over his ears, trying to remember the life he'd left behind — back in L.A. seventeen years before. He was young then and he thought he ruled the world. Attitude was everything and it bought him what he wanted: money, women, cars, and most of all respect on the street. He had his friends and nobody messed with him, not more than once. He was tough, violent sometimes, but he wasn't a killer, like some of the guys he met in the joint. He leaned back in his seat and pictured himself as he was then, hanging outside a club with his gang, bling around his neck, a hot woman in a slinky black dress on his arm. King of his own little world.

"You was a big dawg back in the day," McGrath said, "and now you think you'll pick up where you left off. Swagger down those same streets and them gangbangers'll lay down their guns and fall at your feet."

Ruffin kept his mind on the scene from his past: a tense standoff with a rival gang, a sudden fight that ended with him tossing one of the cringing fools through a store window.

"You think by going in the joint you bought respect," McGrath said. "You didn't snitch, you didn't eat shit. You stayed alive by picturing the day you'd go back and those punks'd step aside for you, show you the respect you deserve."

Ruffin opened his eyes and saw McGrath grinning at him like a jackass. "But you been fooling yourself, Ruffin," McGrath said. "They don't respect you out there anymore. It's a different world and you got no place in it. You're a dinosaur, is what you are. They'd just as soon shoot you as look at you. In fact that's probably what they're planning to do the minute you get off the bus. They ain't gonna let you back on the street."

Ruffin turned toward McGrath with a desperate, violent eagerness. He couldn't listen to this any longer without reacting. "I'm out and they're gonna respect me."

"Then you better plan on killing them before they kill you."

"I ain't killing nobody." Ruffin thought about smiling, but stopped himself. "Except maybe you, if you don't shut up."

The bus cruised south on the freeway and they both dozed off. Never at loss for words, McGrath snored garrulously and muttered in his sleep. As he woke up, Ruffin squinted out the window at the setting sun.

"How long is this trip anyway?" he asked, hoping McGrath wouldn't answer.

"Eight hours and ten minutes," McGrath said. "We're almost there."

It was chilly on the bus, but McGrath had the sleeves of his sweatshirt rolled up as if he thought his tattoos would keep him warm. His arms were etched with naked girls, mermaids, cobwebs, batwings, and various card faces, including the queen of hearts. "That one was a mistake," he told Ruffin. "Sort of sends the wrong message, you know what I mean?"

"Long as you ain't got any Aryan Brotherhood shit on there," Ruffin said, squinting at his arms.

"I had a swastika but them neo-Nazi snobs made me scrape it off. They said I was ruining their brand." He rolled down the sleeves and held out his arms to show off his sweatshirt. "Look at us, Ruffin. We don't got dress outs, just these crummy sweats. You know what that means? It means nobody gives enough of a shit about us to send up any real clothes. You got family in L.A.?"

"I got a little boy," Ruffin said. "Not little anymore. He's a teenager by now. Name is Jayden."

"You got a wife?"

"I had a girlfriend. Shanise. She's married now."

"She ever come up to see you on visiting day?"

"Once, a long time ago," Ruffin said. "I never seen the boy. That's gonna change starting tomorrow."

McGrath sighed, like he'd finally stumbled on a profound thought. "You get out of the joint," he said, "you figure, I been punished enough. I want my life back. But here's the thing — you gotta take it back, nobody's gonna give it to you. Them sons of bitches think you owe them something."

"I don't owe shit to nobody," Ruffin said.

"What about Jayden?"

"Don't you worry about Jayden. I'll do the right thing for Jayden." Ruffin said that but he didn't really know what he meant. What could he do for Jayden? He didn't have any money, a job or even a place to live. He couldn't offer Jayden a home, just some time to spend with an ex-con. Can you even bring a kid to a homeless shelter? Maybe McGrath was right — maybe he didn't have what it took to make it on the outside.

McGrath changed the subject. "Me, I've just about gone bankrupt paying my debt to society. I figure that puts me on the same footing as the banks."

It was dark outside. Ruffin closed his eyes and pretended to sleep. McGrath dozed off and snored even more eloquently than before. A blaring truck horn startled them awake. It also startled the little girl, without waking her. She whimpered once or twice and cuddled closer to her mother. Ruffin leaned toward her and smiled. "It's okay," he said. "Just a truck going by."

She was asleep and paid no attention.

The bus cruised down the Santa Ana Freeway into downtown L.A. It left the freeway near Union Station, but the driver took a detour to the shabby neighborhood where the homeless shelter was located. "I got some business to take care of," McGrath said, "then I'm blowing this Third World shithole. Find a pretty woman and go somewhere they'll never look for me. One thing for sure, this time I ain't going back inside."

Things were going on in L.A. that Ruffin and McGrath had no way of knowing about. If they'd known about them they might have stayed on the bus and asked the driver to take them back to San Quentin. But the driver wouldn't have let them do that. He would have made them get off where they were supposed to. That's what he got paid to do.

In that shabby, deserted neighborhood, a black BMW with tinted windows glided to a stop in an unlighted parking lot set back from the street. The driver's side faced the sidewalk, where a dim street light hovered over the misty street. The driver turned off his lights and left the engine running as he waited for the bus.

The bus drove past seedy storefronts and sidewalks peopled with homeless men, drunks, pimps, hookers, teenage thugs. McGrath gazed out the window, shaking his head with concern at what he saw. "This country's gone into the crapper since we been inside, Ruffin," he said. "Look around and all you see is violence, drugs, crime. Not that I got anything against crime per se. But this? Things've gone out of control."

He turned away from the window and stared keenly at Ruffin. "I worry about your son. How can you raise a kid in world like this?"

Ruffin glared back at him. "Don't you worry. I'll look out for my son."

"Maybe I can help you. I'm gonna be staying... at a sister's house, 'til I get my business transacted. I can help you if you stick with me."

Ruffin laughed. "Stick with you? What are you talking about?"

"What I'm thinking—"

"Let me tell you something," Ruffin said. "For the last eight hours I been looking forward to getting off this bus the way I looked forward to getting out of Quentin for seventeen years."

"I'm just saying—"

"McGrath," Ruffin said, still laughing, "you need to understand something: If I never see you again, that'll be way too soon."

McGrath turned back toward the window with an abashed but sly expression, as if he'd been humoring Ruffin all along.

The driver of the black BMW lowered his window to toss out a cigarette. He was a young black man named Alonzo Payne, with light skin, a big nose and a high forehead. He pulled a .45-caliber Glock 21 out of his pocket and switched off the safety. Then he rolled the window back up and waited.

On the bus, the driver looked in his inside mirror as he brought the bus to a stop along the curb. "All right, you two," he shouted to Ruffin and McGrath. "This is where you get off."

Ruffin glanced out the window as the bus stopped. A yellow mist drifted over the sidewalk under a street light. Beyond the sidewalk stood some darkened buildings and an empty lot with one parked car, a black BMW with its engine running and its tinted windows rolled up. No homeless shelter in sight. Ruffin didn't like the idea of staying in a shelter — wasn't it about the same as a jail? — but he had nowhere else to go. He'd grown up in a dozen foster homes with children's shelters in between, and those were about the same as jails too. They didn't beat you as much, unless you dissed them and then you might as well be in San Quentin. When he turned eighteen they couldn't keep him there anymore, but he still had no place to go. No family, and no job either, but there were some brothers in the neighborhood who treated him right, helped him when he needed help, gave him drugs, loaned him money. They were his friends and he could always stay with one of them. Shanise called them a gang but they had no special outfits, no tattoos, no name, they were just a bunch of friends who kept the real gangs off their asses. He earned their respect and became the man they looked up to, because nobody messed with him and he didn't mess with nobody else unless they needed it. The real gangs hated him because he didn't play their game, and so did the cops, for the same reason. He could fight and everybody knew he fought to win. He'd met Shanise when he was nineteen. She was different from anybody he knew. She'd stayed in school and when she graduated she got a job as a clerk at the city water department. She wanted him to go back to school, especially after she got pregnant. He should have listened to her. Instead he did some things he shouldn't have done, made some enemies he shouldn't have made, saw some things he shouldn't have seen. And then he was arrested and the cops threw everything they had at him and his Legal Aid lawyer sold him out for a job in the D.A.'s office and the next thing he knew he was doing hard time in San Quentin. They took his life away from him and he was here to take it back.

McGrath stood up and carefully lifted his garbage bag down from the overhead rack. Everything he owned was in that bag. It wasn't much — in a few days he'd have a lot more, more than he could imagine, but for now this was all he had. He waited for Ruffin to take his bag down and the two of them shuffled toward the front of the bus.

"I got a sister's house I'm staying at," McGrath told the driver. "I ain't sleeping in no shelter."

"I don't care where you sleep," the driver said. "This is where you're getting off."

In the parking lot, the driver's window of the BMW glided open. Alonzo Payne sat back to keep his face out of sight. The barrel of his Glock protruded through the window, pointing toward the bus. He had his instructions. He knew what he had to do.

The little girl and her mother woke up thinking this was their stop. They stood up and hurried down the aisle with their bags, lining up behind McGrath and Ruffin.

"Hey," the driver said to the mother. "You don't get off here."

The mother didn't understand what the driver said. She and the girl kept walking behind Ruffin and McGrath, down into the stairwell and out through the door.

McGrath was the first to step off the bus under the dim street light. Did he sense that something was wrong? Did he notice the BMW and wonder what it was doing there with its engine running? Everything happened so quickly.

Ruffin came out right behind him. He stopped and turned around to help the little girl down. Her mother was following close behind — she stepped into the doorway just as the shots rang out from the BMW.

Three shots, one right after another.

"Get down!" McGrath screamed.

Four shots, five, six. McGrath and Ruffin both went down on the sidewalk. As he fell, Ruffin threw his arms around the girl but she and her mother were hit too. The BMW sped away — as people on the bus later told the police — before anybody knew what happened.

The bus driver snapped the door shut and drove away, leaving the victims sprawled on the sidewalk.

3

Sirens howling in the distance like a pack of wolves — that's how Ruffin remembered it later. A strobing flood of light as the ambulances and police cars claimed a contested patch of concrete in the urban battleground. Boots on the pavement, shouted commands, police radios, the roar of a helicopter overhead. The eerie luminosity of a TV news truck and its ghostlike blonde oracle under the portable spotlights. A quick ride to the Emergency Room and then a frenzy of activity as EMTs and cops rushed the victims inside on gurneys. First the little girl, under an oxygen mask, and then her mother, who was already dead. The girl's name was Luisa Salazar. Nurses and doctors huddled around her, trying to save her life. Ruffin's sweatshirt was soaked in blood but all he had was a flesh wound in his shoulder, no more than he would have expected in a brawl at San Quentin. McGrath lay motionless on a gurney, apparently dead.

When Ruffin's gurney stopped in a small curtained area, he leaned on his elbow to ask the nurse: "That little girl all right?"

"I'm sorry, I can't talk about other patients, sir," the nurse said, peeling back the temporary dressing they'd put on his shoulder in the ambulance. A doctor who looked about fourteen examined the wound and daubed something on it.

Under bright overhead lights in a separate curtained area, a weary resident named Dr. Klein peered down at McGrath's unresponsive body. "His vitals are normal," the nurse said.

The doctor opened one of McGrath's eyelids and it stayed open after his hand came away. "Are you okay, sir? Were you hit?"

McGrath saw lights swaying over him like welcoming angels. "Did I die and go to heaven? Is that where I am?"

"This is the Emergency Room, sir."

McGrath's body stiffened as he relived the attack. "Ruffin!" he shouted. "Get down! They're trying to kill you!"

Half an hour later two plainclothes officers, Detective Julie Morales, 33, trim and attractive, and her partner, Detective Jerry Burke, saggy and bald and close to fifty, arrived at the ER looking for the two cons involved in the bus stop shooting. Routine, or maybe a little more than routine, Morales thought — because what are the odds that a bus just happens to get shot at when two cons fresh out of San Quentin step off it? The detectives stopped to consult a uniformed officer who'd arrived with the ambulance. He pointed them toward the small recovery room where McGrath lay on his gurney ogling nurses who passed in the hall.

By this time Ruffin was in a recovery room of his own, talking to a friendly nurse named Jane Russo, RN. They'd put a big bandage on his shoulder. "You need to lie down in here and rest," the nurse said, "until one of the doctors says you can be discharged."

"I ain't going back out there tonight."

"You'll be safe here," she smiled.

He made an effort to smile back at her as if they were having a normal conversation, but the smile felt strange on his face, like it didn't belong there. He'd been inside so long, he didn't know how to talk to a woman. "You sure about that?"

"I'll make sure of it."

"Thanks."

"Your wound is minor and should heal quickly," she said. "But you'll need to come in tomorrow and have the dressing changed so it doesn't get infected." Her smile dimmed, became a little more distant and bureaucratic, when she remembered the two cops. "Since it's a gunshot wound, you'll have to talk to the police officers before you can go home."

Ruffin showed her his own distant, hollowed-out smile, the kind he reserved for people who expected him to talk to the cops. He'd already seen enough cops for one lifetime. Something told him he'd be seeing a lot more before long.

The nurse stooped down and pulled a black plastic bag out from under the gurney. "I almost forgot," she said. "One of the officers brought this bag in from the ambulance. Is it yours?"

"Yeah, that's mine. Thanks."

"Do you need something to drink? A Coke or something?"

"Sure, thanks. A Coke would be great. Mind if I use the phone?"

"Just to call home? Sure, no problem."

Everything Ruffin owned, which wasn't much, was in that bag. A clean pair of underwear, a pair of socks, a tooth brush, a deck of cards. A Bible. Just then the only thing he cared about was a small card stuck in his Bible where he'd written Shanise's phone number. Calling Shanise wasn't exactly calling home — he didn't have a home — but it was the closest he could come.

He didn't know if Shanise would talk to him or not. She was married, he'd heard, and living out toward the airport. He found the card and dialed her number on the hospital phone.

Shanise was finishing dinner with her husband Derek and her son Jayden, who was also Ruffin's son. Jayden was seventeen and Ruffin had never laid eyes on him. He had the kind of hair style and clothes and attitude that usually went along with being in a gang. Derek was an ex-Marine who lifted weights and drove for Federal Express. He didn't like gangs and he didn't like Jayden's attitude any more than his hair style or his clothes.

"Hello?" Shanise answered.

"Shanise, it's me," Ruffin said. "Kenny. I'm out on parole."

She made something up to keep Derek from knowing who it was. "We don't need any of those. Thanks anyway."

"I want to see you," Ruffin said. "And Jayden."

"No, sorry, I told you we don't need any."

"You still work for the water department?" Ruffin was desperate to keep her on the phone. He didn't know what he'd do if she hung up on him. "I'll meet you tomorrow," he said.

"Don't call again."

"At that place on Beverly we used to eat lunch at. Polly's. Be there at noon."

She hung up. "Telemarketer."

Derek glared at her skeptically, as if he knew who it was. "You're way too polite to those people," he said. "You ought to just hang up on them."

Jayden pushed his plate away and headed for the door.

"Hey," Derek said. "Where do you think you're going?"

"I got shit to do."

"Yeah, well I don't like the shit you do, or the fact that you call it shit, even though that's probably what it is. And I don't like the so-called friends you do it with. You're going to end up dead of an overdose or shot by the cops."

"You don't know my friends," Jayden glared back.

"I know enough about them to know they're using drugs, probably selling them, carrying guns and on their way to jail if they survive long enough to go to jail."

"You got it all wrong. It ain't about drugs, it's about respect. You wouldn't understand."

He stalked out, with Derek glowering after him. Shanise muttered an excuse to go upstairs.

Three miles away in South Los Angeles, Alonzo Payne, the young man who'd greeted the bus from San Quentin with a burst of gunfire, raced his black BMW down a rutted street in a panic. He'd just been told on his phone that he botched up what was supposed to be an easy job. When he sped away from that bus, four bodies lay in a heap on the sidewalk, but somehow those stiffs must have come back to life, three of them anyway. Only one of them was dead and that was some woman he wasn't even supposed to be shooting at. Not his lucky day.

Two teenagers named DeWayne and Earl waited for Alonzo in front of a bar called Wellington's. He pulled over to the curb and they climbed into the BMW, grinning, cracking jokes, trying to act cool, but they were scared shitless when he handed them a pair of Glock 21's. Heavy, serious semi-automatic weapons like they'd never held before. "Better tell me now if you ready for this," he said. "Cause if you ain't—"

"I'm ready," DeWayne said in his high-pitched, cracking voice. He sounded like a dog being whipped.

"I'm ready," Earl said, so low Alonzo could hardly hear him.

"Okay," Alonzo said. "That man's going down. Hear me? He's going down."

4

The two detectives, Morales and Burke, barged into Ruffin's recovery room without knocking. "Mr. Ruffin," the woman said, flashing her badge, "I'm Detective Morales of the LAPD. This is Detective Burke."

Ruffin lowered his eyes like he always did when cops looked at him. The nurse had warned him about these cops but he still didn't want to see them. Couldn't he get through his first day out of jail without being hassled by the cops?

"We know who you are, you and McGrath," the one called Burke said.

"San Quentin informed us they were sending you down on the bus," Morales said evenly. She was a good looking woman, a light-skinned Hispanic with coal-black eyes and hair. She had her black eyes on his bandaged shoulder. "How are you feeling?"

"I'm okay," Ruffin said. "Minor flesh wound. How's the little girl?"

"She's in the ICU," Morales said. "Her mother's dead."

"I'm sorry."

"You're gonna be," Burke snarled. He sounded like he learned his lines at the bad cop academy. Ruffin glared at him, saw a flabby, faded weasel with thin reddish hair, eyes the color of piss, who would have been in a desk job by now if he wasn't too stupid to find the desk.

"You can't blame me," Ruffin said. "I'm the one they was shooting at."

Burke snorted like he'd thought of something smart to say. "You're like a nuclear plant, Ruffin," he said. "You kill people just by being within a mile of them."

Ruffin ignored him and looked at Morales. "What do you want from me?"

"We were hoping you could help us," she said, trying to keep it friendly. "Did you see the shooters? Do you have any idea who they were?"

"I didn't see nothing."

The nurse walked in with Ruffin's Coke, stepped in front of the cops and handed it to him like it was medicine, then stood waiting for him to drink it. "These cops are bothering me," he told her.

She eyed the cops disapprovingly and they headed toward the door. Then Burke stopped and turned around. "You have an appointment tomorrow with your parole agent," he said. "You better keep it."

"Don't they make an exception for getting shot?" Ruffin asked. He was feeling a little cocky now that they were leaving.

"You've used up all your exceptions, Ruffin," Burke said. "From now on, there's nothing you can do that won't be wrong. You got that?"

Morales smiled and handed him her card. She had a nice smile and he could see why she was the good cop, or would have been if there was any such thing as a good cop. "Call me if you remember anything," she said. "We're going to find who did this."

"Not if I find him first," Ruffin said.

"You better stay the hell out of the way," Burke warned him.

"Somebody shoots at me, they better hit the target. Not some little girl I'm helping off a bus."

"Let us do our job, Mr. Ruffin," Morales said.

"Nobody does this to me."

They stared at him a few seconds like he was some kind of exotic animal and walked out. The nurse asked, "Are you in some kind of trouble, sir?"

He let out a little laugh but didn't answer. "Thanks for the Coke. Say, that other guy that come in with me. He shot up pretty bad?"

"No. There's nothing wrong with him."

"Nothing at all?"

She shook her head.

"Damn," Ruffin said.

"I think he just wanted a ride in the ambulance."

On the street around the corner from the hospital, Alonzo parked the BMW and ordered DeWayne and Earl out. They milled around on the sidewalk trying not to think about the guns in their pockets, but thinking about them anyway, telling themselves it was no big deal carrying a piece, it was all in a day's work and it made you a man. Earl was eighteen, De-Wayne nineteen. Both of them had stopped going to school when they were fifteen and now they smoked crack every day if Alonzo gave it to them. The days he didn't give it to them were bad days.

Alonzo climbed out of the car holding his phone to his ear. "Whatever shit happened at that bus stop ain't gonna happen again," he said into the phone. "Five minutes from now, that dude is a dead man."

The three of them slouched toward the emergency room entrance. Alonzo quiet and determined, DeWayne and Earl joking around, laughing, being cool.

They were on their way to kill a man. It was no big deal.

In the hospital corridor Ruffin could hear McGrath's voice, at first sort of low and growling, then becoming clearer: "...And I pounded them sons of bitches so hard they was spitting out their teeth and begging for mercy before they crawled back to their car."

McGrath stopped talking and almost fell off his gurney when Ruffin walked into the room. "Who you talking to?" Ruffin asked him.

He peered around like there might be somebody else in the room. It was eight feet square and the gurney took up seven feet of it. "There was a nurse in here a minute ago. I guess she must of—"

"I don't want to hear a load of shit," Ruffin said. "I just want to know if you saw who did the shooting."

"I didn't see shit, just a hail of bullets out of a car window."

"Were they white or black?"

"I told you I didn't see shit."

"Don't bullshit me. Why'd you look so scared when I walked in here?"

"Okay, it was a black guy, but I don't want the word to get out that I saw anybody, understand?"

"What'd he look like?"

"I don't know. I told you—"

Ruffin grabbed his arm and twisted it almost out of the socket. "What'd he look like?"

"Light skin, big forehead, big nose. Mid-twenties, maybe younger."

"Just one of them?"

"I told you, I didn't see shit."

"What kind of car?"

"Black BMW."

When Ruffin stepped back into the hospital corridor he saw three men walking toward him with their hands in their pockets. One of them fit the description of the shooter he'd just heard from McGrath: light skin, big forehead, big nose, mid-twenties. It was Alonzo Payne. The other two were Earl and DeWayne. They looked like a couple of kids on their way to visit their grandma in the hospital.

Ruffin jumped back into McGrath's room and slammed the door. But the men must have seen him. Within five seconds they were pounding and kicking the door and trying to break it down.

"Open the damn door!" Alonzo shouted.

5

Suddenly the pounding stopped and Ruffin heard a woman's voice trying to calm the attackers. It must have been one of the nurses. "How can I help you?" she asked.

"We're hoping visiting hours ain't over," Alonzo said.

"We don't want no visitors," Ruffin yelled through the door.

"Trying to get a little rest in here," McGrath added.

"Who are you here to see?" the nurse asked Alonzo.

"Man in there," he said. "He's expecting us."

"There are two men in there," the nurse said. "Why do you need to see them right now?"

"They only got a couple minutes to live."

They shoved their way past the nurse and resumed their assault on the door, pushing it halfway open as Ruffin tried to hold it shut. The nurse ran down the hall.

Ruffin went on the attack before they could pull out their guns. He let the door fly open and grabbed the nearest one — it was DeWayne — and pulled him down by the hair, then kicked his head hard enough to put him out. He ducked behind McGrath's gurney and shoved it toward the other two, knocking them backwards, pinning them against the wall. Then he punched Alonzo in the face and thumped Earl's head against the wall. The pain in his wounded shoulder reminded him that this was the second time he'd been attacked. He punched Alonzo again. "This for the first time," he said. "And this" — he punched him harder — "is for right now." He grabbed

Earl's hair and cracked his head against Alonzo's. "Next time I see your ass," he said, "the dudes with a couple minutes to live gonna be you."

McGrath lay on the gurney as flat and motionless as a corpse. When Ruffin finished pummeling Alonzo and Earl, McGrath jumped off and bent down to search the unconscious DeWayne, slipping the Glock 21 out of his pocket before following Ruffin down the hall.

Panic and pandemonium had taken over the ER at the first sign of violence, and now it spilled outside, carrying Ruffin and McGrath along with most of the hospital staff out to the circular driveway and the street. The uniformed cops left behind by Morales and Burke had disappeared.

McGrath grabbed a taxi and pulled Ruffin in beside him on the back seat. The driver was a bald, nervous Indian man in his fifties who seemed in no hurry to go anywhere.

"L.A. County Hospital," McGrath said, "and make it quick. We're hurt."

The driver smiled beatifically. "This is not an ambulance, sir," he said.

"It's gonna be a hearse if you don't take us where we want to go. And speed it up."

The taxi glided away as Ruffin watched out the rear window. Alonzo and his friends had run out behind them and must have seen them escaping in the taxi. After a couple of blocks Ruffin saw the black BMW swerving through the traffic behind them. "I should've killed them when I had the chance," he said.

"Good rule of thumb," McGrath said, "don't kill anybody on your first day out on parole. Makes Corrections look bad, and they don't like that."

McGrath poked the driver in the shoulder. "See that Beamer coming up behind us? Step on the gas and get away from it as fast as you can."

"I don't do car chases, sir," the driver said.

McGrath pulled out DeWayne's Glock and jammed it into the driver's neck. "Like hell you don't."

The cab sped up, but the driver hit the brakes at the next traffic light.

"What the hell are you stopping for?" McGrath asked.

"I obey all applicable traffic laws."

The BMW came up behind them and crunched into their rear bumper as they stopped. Then it backed up for a better firing position. Ruffin caught a glimpse of Alonzo and Earl leaning out with their guns just before the taxi's rear window exploded into a million pieces. He wanted to jump out and run but he knew he'd never make it. They'd gun him down right there on the street and nobody'd even know he was back in L.A. He'd never see Jayden or Shanise or anybody else he knew. The cops would haul his body to the morgue and toss him in the crematorium and that would be the end of it.

The attack seemed to be going on forever when that stupid peckerwood McGrath, bless his hillbilly heart, opened his door and rolled out, crouching down with his head and shoulders low so he could fire back and make the attackers duck for cover. Was Ruffin supposed to follow him out of the cab? He was too big, he couldn't crouch that low, and he didn't have a gun — it would be suicide to do that while these fools were shooting at each other. If McGrath kept shooting, maybe the two of them could run out and disappear in the night. But instead McGrath reached up and opened the front door — that must have been his plan all along — and slid into the driver's seat with his head down, pushing the driver down on the floor. He threw the cab in gear and raced away, laughing like a madman.

"There will be an additional charge for any and all damage to the vehicle," the driver said, trembling on the floor.

Ruffin wished he'd jumped out when he had the chance. He'd have been better off in the crematorium than riding in that taxi with McGrath at the wheel. Alonzo and Earl were close behind them, firing out of both sides of their car. Then all of a sudden a cop car joined the chase behind the BMW with its lights flashing and its siren wailing. When Alonzo turned to escape, the cop car chased after him and disappeared into the night. McGrath whipped around a few corners and before long they were cruising below the speed limit on South Vermont, looking like an ordinary L.A. taxi — full of bullet holes and with the back window shot out.

They stopped at a light and McGrath tossed the gun out between a couple of burnt-out junk cars. They could hear the sirens howling back in the direction they came from. McGrath leaned over and opened the door on the passenger side. "All right you quivering piece of chicken shit," he told the driver, "you've reached your destination."

The driver crawled into the street and they drove away, taking it slow and stopping at all the lights. It was a poor neighborhood with a lot of bars and convenience stores and painted stucco houses that looked like tiny junk yards with cinder-block walls and razor wire fences around them. In a few blocks they stopped in front of a playground crowded with Hispanic teenagers, who stared at them like they'd just arrived from another planet. McGrath tossed the car keys on the front seat as they climbed out of the taxi. "We better ditch this gas hog before we get stuck with the payments. Those kids'll make sure nobody finds it in one piece."

He led Ruffin around a corner squinting at house numbers until they came to a shabby bungalow with broken windows patched with duct tape and knee-high weeds for a front lawn. There was no porch light and no lights on inside. On the front porch McGrath groped under a flower pot and when he found a key he unlocked the door. Inside, he prowled around locking the doors and windows and lowering the blinds. "This place smells worse than Quentin," he said. "But don't open any windows. And don't turn on any lights till we get the shades down."

"Where's your sister?" Ruffin asked.

"She's out of town. I thought I told you that. I think—"

Ruffin grabbed McGrath and pushed him against a wall, rattling a bunch of plaques and pictures that hung there. "I'm done listening to your bullshit, McGrath. You don't have a sister that lives in this neighborhood."

"Well, I said 'a' sister, didn't I? I didn't exactly say my sister."

"Whose sister is she then?"

"A guy in the joint named Grijalva. I gave him an ounce of weed and he told me where his sister lives."

"He told you where his own sister lives?"

"She testified against him at his murder trial. He's sort of hoping I'll kill her."

Ruffin bounced McGrath against the wall and some of the pictures crashed down. He wanted to strangle him or peel the rest of the skin off his head or at least knock his straight white prison teeth down his snake-encircled throat.

"Don't worry," McGrath croaked. "She's on vacation down in Mexico." He straightened his clothes, trying to recover his lost dignity. "Won't be back for a week. Gives you and me a chance to get organized."

"You stupid shit! What are you getting me into?"

"Is that any way to talk to a man who just saved your life? And who's offering you a place to spend the night?"

"I could've stayed at the shelter."

"What shelter?"

"The shelter I was supposed to stay at."

"Did you see a shelter? All I saw was a hail of bullets."

"There's a shelter somewhere and that's where I'm going."

"Trust me, Ruffin, the first time you show your ass in that shelter somebody's gonna shoot it full of holes. Haven't you been paying attention? Somebody's trying to kill you. Without me by your side you'd be at room temperature by now."

Ruffin backed McGrath into the kitchen. There was a sink, stove, refrigerator — the usual stuff — but nothing within reach either one of them could use as a weapon. They stood facing each other in a momentary truce.

"This ain't exactly what I had in mind for my retirement," McGrath said calmly. "But we got to make the best of it, don't we? We're in this together now."

"In what together?"

"You heard what that punk said. 'Them dudes only got a couple minutes to live.' He was talking about us — both of us."

"Shut up."

McGrath laughed in his face. "You owe me."

"I don't owe you shit."

"Face it, Ruffin, you'll never get rid of me. We're practically joined at the hip."

6

The next morning was as bright and sunny as a morning in L.A. can be. On a day like this, if you plan on getting out of your car, you count your blessings: no lung-scorching smog, eye-scouring sulfur, or glacier-liquidating ozone. But if you're the average person you never leave your car. You just crawl out of bed and stagger out to resume your life sentence of sitting in traffic on the freeway. You might tune in the weather on the radio, just to confirm that today will be like every other day, but that's as far as your interest in the outside world goes. If yesterday was any different, you'd have forgotten it by now. This is L.A.

Julie Morales arrived at the division police station at the usual time and cautiously parked her Ford Focus in the employee lot. She lived by herself, not because she wanted to but because she couldn't live any other way. Her mother was out in San Bernardino, too far to commute from, and if you lived with her you couldn't hold a job — she had so many health complaints you had to spend all your time dealing with them. Her dad couldn't take it any more, he'd fled to Chicago long ago. She'd lost her older brother, who'd inspired her to be a cop. She loved her little sister but not the soap opera she starred in, or the treacherous boyfriends, jealous girlfriends, overbearing bosses and scheming co-workers who played supporting roles. Being a cop was drama enough, even with a partner like Burke, who would have spent his time counting the days to retirement if he could count that high. She'd had a live-in boyfriend for a while — an addiction counselor named Leo who hated his clients even more than the system that created them — until she caught him smoking crack in her apartment. He was lucky she didn't arrest him. Sometimes she wondered if she'd given up on life, at least the kind of life that was available to her. She lived by herself and drove a red Ford Focus and tried to do a good job with her detective work even though nobody else gave a damn about it, least of all her boss, Lieutenant Hague (rhymes with vague), whose only concern was to make sure she didn't detect anything.

She noticed Hague's awkward form when she stood up from her car, shambling across the parking lot with Burke, the two of them muttering to each other like a couple of pigeons. Hague was a grizzled veteran who always tried to seem tougher than he was and never succeeded. It's hard to look tough when your Adam's apple is bigger than your chin. He acted almost frightened when Morales caught up with them. "You hear what happened at Cal Medical Center after you left last night?" he grunted without saying hello. The three of them continued walking toward the station entrance.

"After we left?"

"Some gangbangers showed up at the E.R. trying to get at those two cons you talked to. Staged quite a brawl in one of the recovery rooms. And then they ran out."

"The gangbangers?" Morales asked.

"The gangbangers *and* the cons. Ran out before anybody could stop them."

"We left two uniforms in the E.R.," Morales said. "Why didn't they stop them?"

"Probably on their break," Hague winced. "What did the cons say when you talked to them? Did they see the shooters?"

"They claimed they didn't see anything."

"You believe them?"

"I'm not sure I believed McGrath," she said. "He seemed—"

"Don't waste your time on that moron. The other guy, Ruffin—he's the one you need to focus on."

"Ruffin said he's going after the shooters."

Hague's phone buzzed as they reached the station entrance. He pulled it out of his pocket and let it buzz. "That's your lead, then," he said. "Find Ruffin and don't take your eyes off him. He'll lead you to the scumbags that shot Luisa Salazar."

"Right," Morales agreed.

Hague nodded at his phone. "This'll be the Commissioner calling. He's gonna want to know why we haven't made an arrest. I'm going to tell him we're moving to Plan B."

"Plan B?" Burke said as if he suddenly woke up.

"You know what Plan B is, Burke. No more screw-ups."

Morales and Burke left Hague on the steps with his phone and walked past the security desk and up the stairs to the office. "I guess Hague's had some prior dealings with McGrath," Morales observed.

"The guy's a piece of work," Burke said. "He's talked his way in and out of San Quentin so many times they call him The Cat Came Back."

"What's that supposed to mean?"

"Remember the old song? *The cat came back. We thought he was a goner but the cat came back.*"

Morales laughed. "Wasn't he involved in that human trafficking case a few years ago? You remember. Some Russian strangled an underage prostitute and disappeared."

"Yeah, I think he was."

"Well, we know where the cat's going to be at one o'clock this afternoon. He has an appointment with his parole agent. Harold Chung."

"I hope he likes Chinese food," Burke said. "And shit. He'll be eating a lot of shit too."

"I wonder if he'll bring Ruffin along. His appointment's at the same time."

"I'll give Chung a call. You heard what the lieutenant said. No more screw-ups."

Outside on the steps, Hague stood to one side gritting his teeth as he listened to the Commissioner fulminating. He couldn't see him, of course, but he could picture him in his office downtown: a jowly sycophant in a shiny blue suit, parked behind a massive oak desk holding a book as he barked into a speaker phone. The Commissioner was always reading a book; he fancied himself an intellectual, although (as Hague well knew) he was much more than that. Hague had learned that to hold the Commissioner at bay he had to find out what he was reading and sound interested, even if it was some stupid shit that no cop would waste his time on. Of course the Commissioner wasn't really a cop, more like a politician or even, when you came down to it, a gangster, which is what all the politicians were if you came down to it. Did he really read those books? Or was that just for show, to impress the overeducated reporters when they interviewed him in his office? That was all he cared about—what they said about him on TV and the internet. The city could have been sacked like ancient Rome, crated up and carried away — maybe it already had been — by every drug cartel from Mexico to Moscow and the Commissioner wouldn't have given three shits as long as he looked good on the news.

"You got anything for me yet?" he growled at Hague.

"Not yet," Hague said. "Give me a couple more hours."

"Have you seen today's news? Try to imagine what tomorrow's is going to look like if you screw this up."

"That won't happen, sir," Hague said. "We've moved to Plan B."

"Plan B? Good. Keep me informed."

"By the way, Commissioner," Hague asked, "what are you reading these days?"

"Thanks for asking," the Commissioner said. "I'm reading *Being and Nothingness,* by Jean-Paul Sartre."

"Great book," Hague said.

"You've read it?"

"Sure, all the guys have read it. Sartre is one of the all-time favorites in this division. Right up there with Michael Connelly."

7

Ruffin woke up in his clothes in a small musty bedroom in Grijalva's sister's house and gazed out the window at the hazy sunlight drifting over a patch of overgrown weeds, cactuses and scrubby broken trees. A rat sniffed its way around an overflowing garbage can in front of the house next door. Empty beer and liquor bottles and rolled-up dirty diapers littered the space between the houses. Welcome to the real world. Ruffin felt shitty but he told himself he ought to feel great. It was the day he'd been looking forward to for seventeen years, his first day of freedom. Freedom to do what? he wondered. His shoulder ached as if he'd been shot. Then he remembered: he had been shot, getting off that bus, before his feet even touched the ground.

In the living room he found McGrath guzzling from a bottle of Wild Turkey as he shoved Grijalva's sister's belongings — a flat-screen TV, a stereo boom box, small kitchen appliances — into boxes and grocery bags. The front door stood open and an old car was backed up to it with the trunk lid up. "What's all this shit?" he asked McGrath.

"Collateral," McGrath said. "Grab anything we can pawn and put it in the car."

"Where'd you get the car?"

"It's the sister's. I found it out back. She won't be needing it anymore."

He offered Ruffin a swig of the Wild Turkey, but Ruffin waved it aside. The night before, they'd consumed every drop of alcohol in the house along with some moldy cheese, a box of stale Ritz crackers and five cans of Chef Boyardee ravioli, which tasted worse than the food in San Quentin. At the moment, throwing up seemed like a better idea than drinking more booze.

McGrath must have had a stronger stomach. He'd gone out for the Wild Turkey before Ruffin woke up. "Let's take a look at that shoulder," he said.

Ruffin sat on a chrome-and-vinyl kitchen chair while McGrath unwrapped his bandage and poked at the wound. "Looks pretty ugly," McGrath said, "just like the rest of you. What did the nurse say to do?"

"She said come back today and get the bandage changed."

"The hell with that," McGrath said. "You're a dead man if you show your face in that hospital, you know that. Here" — he poured some Wild Turkey on the wound as Ruffin gritted his teeth — "this'll heal you right up." He wrapped the dirty bandage back around Ruffin's shoulder, securing it with some duct tape he found in a kitchen drawer. Then he held up the bottle to show Ruffin how much of the Wild Turkey he'd used to treat him. "No wonder health care is so damned expensive," he said. "This shit cost me $27.99 plus tax."

McGrath tossed a few more items into a cardboard box and carried them out to the car. "First thing we need is some cash," he told Ruffin. "Then some decent threads and a couple of phones. You can't live in the modern world without a phone." He dumped the box into the open trunk and came back for more, emptying the kitchen drawers and yanking pictures off the walls.

"Ain't that enough?" Ruffin asked.

"It takes a lot of cash to be a law-abiding citizen in this town."

Ruffin found a framed picture of a good-looking brunette in a bikini, striking a sexy pose with a come-hither smile. "This must be Grijalva's sister," he said, taking the picture down from the wall.

"Toss it in," McGrath said. "She won't be needing that anymore neither."

Ruffin handed the picture over and McGrath paused a few seconds to size up the sister. "Not bad, huh?" he said. "Grijalva didn't tell me what a hot number his sister was." He shoved the picture into a grocery bag with some other stuff.

"Why'd she testify against him?" Ruffin asked.

"What?"

"The sister. Why'd she testify against Grijalva at his murder trial?"

"He murdered their mother."

Ruffin followed McGrath out to the car. "You knew this psycho?"

McGrath nodded as he tossed the bag into the trunk. "Nicest guy you'd ever want to meet."

Ruffin had spent most of the night lying awake wondering what he'd do next. He hadn't counted on getting shot before he was off the bus, or ambushed in the emergency room, or chased like a dog through the streets of L.A. McGrath was right — the country'd really gone into the crapper since he went inside. Naturally, like McGrath said (and he hated to admit that anything McGrath said was right), there were guys out there who didn't want to see him back on the street. Afraid he'd cramp their style, crowd their turf, move in on their game, whatever. They knew his reputation and they didn't want him around, no matter what he planned to do. He could guess their names without even asking. That Alonzo asshole wasn't who he needed to worry about — the kid was still in daycare when he went inside. Who was Alonzo working for? — that was the question. Also like McGrath said (and this was getting annoying, basing all his thoughts on the sayings of that peckerwood), he wasn't the man he used to be. He could still kick ass but how much ass could you kick after seventeen years of working in a laundry and eating prison food? There was a whole new generation of wise guys, gangbangers, punks and all around badasses that probably wanted to make a name for themselves by putting him in the ground. The funny thing was, he wouldn't have been a threat to them if they'd just left him alone. All he wanted was a fresh start — he wanted to see Jayden, spend as much time with him as he could — but between the cops and the criminals it didn't look like he was going to get a chance. If they'd left him alone he might have moved on, hitched a ride somewhere and never come back. But instead they met him at the bus from San Quentin and tried to take him out. Nobody was getting away with that shit.

Trailing a cloud of black exhaust, Grijalva's sister's car — it was a battered 1980s Cadillac, sea-green two-door, no hubcaps, that burned a quart of oil with every tank of gas — sailed down busy streets lined with off-brand gas stations and body shops and cut-rate liquor stores and immigrant strip malls, McGrath swigging Wild Turkey from the bottle as he drove, sailing through most of the red lights and tossing the finger at anyone who didn't like it. They found a pawn shop in a strip mall and lugged in the flat-screen TV and the boom box and all the bags and boxes full of the sister's crap. The cheapskate owner barely gave them enough to cover their gas money — McGrath considered using what he gave them to buy a gun to shoot him with — but it was better than nothing. On the way out McGrath grabbed an old set of golf clubs in a leather golf bag and walked out without paying for them.

They left the pawn shop with a spring in their step and moseyed down to a Salvation Army thrift shop that offered a selection of outmoded suits, shirts and accessories, most of which they tried on before finding the ones they wanted. In their new outfits (which must have been donated by sleazy real-estate operators in the 1980s) they looked more like ex-cons than ever. Next was a cheap electronics store, where they picked up a couple of burner phones. "How do you use these damn things?" Ruffin asked as they walked back to the car. Cell phones were a new thing since he went to prison.

"The hell if I know," McGrath said. "We'll figure it out."

When they reached the car, McGrath opened the trunk and moved some of the junk around to make room for the golf bag. "What you doing with them golf clubs?" Ruffin asked.

"I thought I'd practice a little," McGrath said. "Next time I go inside, I'm opting for one of them country club joints. Lompoc, they got a 18-hole course."

Ruffin had always wondered about that. "What you gotta do to get in those places?"

"White collar crime," McGrath said. "Why do you think I'm working on my GED?"

He tossed the golf bag in the trunk and the two of them climbed into the car. McGrath fiddled with the radio until he found a country music station. The car began to fill up with exhaust.

"What I need is a gun," Ruffin said.

"Wipe that thought from your mind and flush it down the toilet," McGrath said. "It's a felony for an ex-felon to own, possess, or have custody or control of any firearm, or any ammunition that was transported through interstate commerce. California Penal Code, Section 29800(a)."

"You got the section memorized?"

"You better memorize it too," McGrath said, "or you'll be back inside quicker'n a turd in a tornado." He groped under the seat for a tire iron and tossed it over to Ruffin. "Carry this instead. You never know when you might need to fix a flat."

In a minute they were fishtailing back onto the busy street, tires squealing, exhaust billowing, as McGrath turned up the country music and thwacked its beat on the steering wheel. "You gonna go after them sons of bitches that shot you?" he asked Ruffin.

"Somebody's gotta do it," Ruffin said.

McGrath laughed. "Somebody's gotta do it? What do you think this is? A cowboy movie?"

"That little girl could've been Jayden."

"Ruffin" — McGrath had the bad habit, as he was driving, of turning his head all the way to the right and looking straight at you when he talked — "I know you don't like my sage advice, but I'm gonna give it to you anyway." A garbage truck stopped in front of them and he had to slam on his brakes to avoid a crash. "The best thing you could do for Jayden is keep your ass out of jail." McGrath gave the truck driver the finger and leaned on his horn. "Not that you got a snowball's chance in hell of doing that."

Ruffin looked away, wrestling with the truth of McGrath's advice while pretending to brush it aside. The country music was really pissing him off. It reminded him of those Aryan Brotherhood skinheads in Quentin with their Nazi tattoos. He reached over and snapped off the radio.

"Before you go hatching any crimes," McGrath said, "you better meet your parole agent. That'll show you what you're up against."

"I gotta see Shanise at noon."

"No problem. We're getting to Chung's early, when he don't expect us."

"Okay," Ruffin said. "Long as I got time to see Shanise at noon."

"This meeting is important, Ruffin. It's when you're going to find out how the parole system works."

They were in a bustling commercial district where most of the signs were in Chinese or Korean. McGrath turned the country music back on, Ruffin changed it to R&B, McGrath changed it back to country and cranked up the volume, at all times keeping his eyes on Ruffin as the car veered from side to side. "What this is," McGrath said, "is a case of mass incarceration. I'm a victim of it too."

"What are you talking about?"

"Have you noticed that prisons are the only industry left in this shithole state? I'm what they call a serial lifer so I know how it works. When you're in for a felony, they always let you out a little early, just to get you in the parole system. Say you get 24 months for breaking and entering. They let you out after 23 and put you on parole for three years. Then after a few weeks you do something to piss off your parole agent — it don't have to be a crime — and you're back inside for another six months."

McGrath had to hit the brakes again. Ruffin reached over and snapped the radio off. He held his hand over the button to keep McGrath from touching it again, and pointed toward the windshield with his other hand. "Would you look where you're going?"

"I know exactly where I'm going. I been here before."

Ruffin wanted to open the door and jump out.

"You do the six months," McGrath went on, "so now you've done 29 months on a 24-month sentence, and the last six months don't count toward your sentence or your parole time. That pisses you off so much, when they let you out you can't help telling your parole agent to go to hell. He puts you back in and when you get out again you still got three years to go."

They lurched into a cheap strip mall featuring check cashing services, taco joints, massage parlors and flat-rate divorce lawyers.

"Bottom line," McGrath said, "you can get out of jail, but you never get out of parole."

8

On a Belair hillside overlooking the city, Bob and Joanne Waterson, a wealthy married couple in their early sixties, lounged by the pool behind their mansion, enjoying the fine Southern California weather as they did every day. Bob was a savvy African-American who'd grown up on the streets of what was then called South Central L.A., carving himself a place in the world that nobody would ever be allowed to take away from him. Joanne was an Irish-German girl from the suburbs of Chicago who had trained as an emergency room nurse. Happily married for thirty-three years, the couple had three grown daughters and six beautiful grandchildren. Joanne, with a full head of white hair that had once been dark brown (Bob liked to call her his platinum blonde), sat knitting a pair of socks for their oldest grandson, who lived in Colorado. Bob scanned the sports section of the *L. A. Times* for news of the NBA playoffs. Both sipped their mid-day margaritas, dipping tortilla chips in a bowl of guacamole prepared by their Guatemalan cook. That afternoon they looked forward to a visit from two of their grandchildren who would come over to play in the pool. The pool boy, Olaf, who lived in a cabana along the back wall, was busy skimming leaves and other debris off the water so it would be ready for them. He was a muscular Swede from Minnesota with vacant eyes and a killer tan that only pool boys, life guards and surfers could afford. When the grandchildren arrived, the Watersons would ask Olaf to stay in his cabana watching TV while they enjoyed some family time and forgot about business concerns. They'd remain out here on the patio until dark and probably do the same thing tomorrow, sipping margaritas and savoring their views of the city and the ocean as they monitored their business over the phone. From their poolside lounge chairs they ran a criminal empire that extended up and down the coast and east to Las Vegas. Among their prize possessions were two Indian tribes, a U.S. Senator and a significant portion of the LAPD.

Bob's phone rang and he learned about the botched assassination attempt of the night before. "How did you let that happen?" he demanded. "Who were you using for this hit?"

"If anybody can take care of this, it ought to be them," Joanne said, shaking her head.

Bob blocked the phone with his hand and reassured Joanne: "He says they'll get it done today."

"They damn well better," she said. "I don't want to have to send Olaf down there. Not today anyway."

"You going somewhere in the Maserati?"

"It's not that. He hasn't finished cleaning the pool. The kids are coming over."

Bob put the phone back to his ear, and the more he listened, the angrier he got. "Who let that moron out of jail?"

"That's what I'd like to know," Joanne chimed in.

"The Parole Board, he says," Bob told Joanne. "Under the regulations or some shit."

"This is like arguing with customer service," Joanne said. "I spend half my life on the phone arguing with customer service."

"This parole crap really pisses me off," Bob shouted into the phone. "Can't you do something about those regulations? I'm trying to run a business here."

"Tell him we want our money back," Joanne suggested. "That's what I always tell customer service."

"Good idea," Bob agreed. Then he said into the phone: "When we paid off the judge to send that clown away, we expected that he'd get killed in the joint, or if he didn't, at least he'd serve his full sentence. I feel like we're not getting our money's worth here."

"Yeah, what is this?" Joanne asked. "Some kind of racket?"

At the strip mall, Ruffin and McGrath parked in a row of cars facing a shabby, windowless Chinese restaurant called Hao Yun. The late morning sun glared off the parked cars and made Ruffin want to cover his eyes. On the brick wall a neon sign blinked "Cocktail Lounge" in alternating colors. A giant pudgy-faced waiter with a pock-marked face lurked in the doorway as if he was expecting them.

"This don't look like no parole department to me," Ruffin said.

"This is what Harold Chung calls his field office," McGrath said. "He manages the place for his uncle. You know what Hao Yun means? *Good luck*."

The giant waiter disappeared inside as they climbed out of the car. A blonde, breast-enhanced hooker in halter top, leather mini-skirt and knee-high boots sashayed around the corner from an alley, twirling the long shoulder strap on her tiny handbag.

"Chung runs a string of hookers who just got out on parole," McGrath explained. "He puts them back on the street and takes a cut of their earnings. Says he's getting them back into the labor market. If they want their gate money, they got to blow him. At least we don't have to do that."

The hooker, who looked about forty under her makeup, waited for them with a lewd smile on her face. "I haven't seen you boys around here before," she said. "You just get out?"

"Yeah," McGrath said, stepping close in front of her. "We both just got out of Quentin."

She brushed the back of her hand across his crotch. "Oooh, a hardened criminal! Or are you just glad to see me?"

They all enjoyed a good laugh over that. McGrath tucked a twenty dollar bill behind her white patent-leather belt and patted her ass. "What's your name, sweetheart?"

"I'm Kimberly."

"Nice to meet you, Kimberly. I'm Cat, and this here's my friend Kenny."

"You going in to talk to Chung?" she asked. "Maybe get some of your gate money?"

"That's the plan," McGrath said. He pointed down the alley toward the back parking lot. "Meet you around back in twenty minutes?"

"Just one at a time, boys."

"Don't worry," McGrath said. "Kenny ain't that good a friend. You got a car?"

"You bet," she said with a sweet smile. "I got an apartment too."

The dimly-lit restaurant had an atmosphere of faded menace left over from the seventies, when you could still call a seedy bar a cocktail lounge. A few scattered customers concealed themselves in red leatherette booths, murmuring over cocktails as they lounged. Slow-turning fans chased flies around the ceiling without catching up to them. The giant pudgy-faced waiter stood by the bar, ignoring Ruffin and McGrath in his sloe-eyed gaze.

Harold Chung sat heaped in a corner booth, his enormous bulk stuffed into a suit and tie that made him look like a huge little boy. Beside him stood a pair of rolling oxygen tanks in case he needed to go anywhere. He acted surprised to see the two parolees walk in and approach him as he sat sipping tea. The big waiter, whose name was Felipe, glided next to him like a bodyguard but he waved him aside. Without standing up — he was too fat to stand up — he held out his hand, but it was too far away for Ruffin to shake. He offered them chairs and they sat down across from him.

"The cat came back," Chung smiled.

"You thought he was a goner," McGrath beamed, "but the cat came back."

"I wasn't expecting you until one o'clock."

"I wanted to get started right away on developing good work habits. You know, punctuality and all that shit. Tell your uncle—"

"I haven't seen my uncle in months."

"He owns this place, don't he? Tell him I'm back and I want the money he owes me."

Chung seemed amused by McGrath's fervor. "I'll tell him if I see him. In the meantime—"

"There ain't gonna be any meantime if I don't get my money."

The parole agent took his time spooning sugar into his tea and stirring it. When he looked up he glanced at Felipe, who nodded and slouched toward the kitchen. On his way into the kitchen, he pulled out his phone and dialed a call.

Chung took a sip of tea and set his cup down. "You're getting into the danger zone, Cat," he said. "I could snap my fingers and put you back in the can. Just like that." He tried snapping his fingers but they were too fat and greasy to make any sound. "No amount of money would help you then."

Smiling, he turned to Ruffin as if noticing him for the first time. "You must be Kenny Ruffin. I hope you realize that your friend here isn't a very good role model. You already violated your conditions by not reporting to the shelter—"

"I got shot getting off the bus," Ruffin said.

"I could put you in holding just for that."

"For getting shot?"

"The past has a way of coming back to bite you, doesn't it?"

"I spent seventeen years learning that."

"Well, it's no different out here." Chung sounded friendly but he had a sly, menacing look in his eyes. "I know all about your life before you went inside. What you did, who you knew, what you knew. That's all ancient history, though, isn't it? Now the question is whether you're going to get beyond the past or let it ruin your life."

"You can't put me back in jail for getting shot," Ruffin said.

"Let's get something straight," Chung said, his eyes narrowing. "Until you finish your parole, I own you. That could be three years or it could be a lot longer. It's up to you."

McGrath broke in with a friendly note of explanation. "Did I mention that parole agents are in the same union as the prison guards?" he asked Ruffin. "They don't give a shit what pen you're locked up in, as long as they got the keys."

"Nobody owns me," Ruffin said.

"I'd rather we worked together as partners," Chung smiled. "You want women, you come to me. I've got quite a nice collection. Take your pick and I'll pay them out of your gate money. When you run out of gate money, we can talk about what you can do to earn more."

"I ain't your bitch."

McGrath laughed. "Dream on," he said.

By the time Ruffin and McGrath walked out of the restaurant, a black Toyota Land Cruiser with tinted windows sped toward the strip mall in response to Felipe's phone call, running red lights, cutting off other cars, racing to intercept the two parolees who'd arrived early for their appointments. In the Land Cruiser sat two brawny white guys in their mid-thirties named Strausser and Duvaloy. Strausser sported western jeans with a turquoise belt buckle, a snap-buttoned western shirt and a pair of spit-shined Tony Lama cowboy boots. He looked like a dumbed-down replica of Arnold Schwartzenegger: big jaw, big forehead, slightly slanted eyes. His hat identified him as a fan of the Anaheim Angels. Duvaloy was shorter, quicker and smarter than Strausser. He wore faded jeans, sneakers, a T-shirt and a Dodgers cap. His hat touted the San Francisco Forty-Niners and his T-shirt showed partiality to certain Warner Brothers cartoon characters, specifically Pinky and The Brain.

Duvaloy was driving while Strausser fiddled with his phone. Each carried in his pockets a phone, a pack of cigarettes, a lighter, and a 9-millimeter Beretta with an extra ammunition clip, in case the man they were looking for offered any resistance.

9

Kimberly lounged in her van in the parking lot, waiting for McGrath and Ruffin to leave the restaurant. They'd prance out counting their gate money, the stupid shits — it was barely enough for a blowjob — but for a few minutes they'd think they were rich, eager to throw their cash around. McGrath disgusted her — and she loathed the thought of what she had to do with him. Just what she needed: a stupid, smelly, tattooed redneck, whisky and cigarette smoke on his breath, God knows what in his veins, who hadn't been near a woman for eight years. She'd have to cater to every sick fantasy he'd pumped himself up with while he was jacking off or getting gang raped in San Quentin, and she had to do it with a smile. Her only consolation was that at the end of the day — if not today some other day — she'd have the pleasure of watching him die.

They came out as predicted, happy as pigs in shit as they counted their gate money and added it to their take from the pawn shop. Kimberly waved from her van and they walked over to talk to her. "You get your gate money?" she asked McGrath through the window.

"I sure did, but I ain't about to spend it all in one place."

"I've got a few different places you could spend it on," she said.

He laughed and climbed into the van beside her. "Okay, let's see what you can do."

"What about you?" she asked Ruffin. "Want me to call one of the other girls?"

"I'll get to that later," Ruffin said. "Right now I got something to do." He looked at McGrath. "I need to go meet Shanise."

McGrath tossed him the car keys. "I'll call you later to pick me up."

"If there's anything left of him," Kimberly laughed. She put the van in gear and they took off.

It was quarter to twelve. Ruffin was already late, because Chung had kept them almost an hour, dangling their gate money and acting like he owned them, though he couldn't even stand up from his chair when they finally plucked the cash out of his hand and headed for the door. He hollered after them that he could put their asses back in jail in a heartbeat, but by that time they didn't believe him or give a shit. "I'll be out of this polluted hellhole before that fat sack of shit can get out of his chair," McGrath said as they sailed through the door. "Soon as I get my money I'm headed to Belize. What about you, Ruffin? What're you gonna do next?"

"I ain't decided yet."

And that was the thing: Ruffin couldn't decide what he wanted to do now that he was out. He wished he could say he was done with crime, but crime was all he knew. When you've been a drug dealer, a gang leader, an armed robber and an unlawful possessor of firearms, and you've spent seventeen years in San Quentin, what are you going to do next? Become an insurance adjuster? He needed to talk to Shanise, find out when he could see Jayden. He hoped she wouldn't give him any shit about that. He even wondered, deep down, if maybe she'd want to come back with him. Who was this husband she'd hooked up with? Was he for real, or just a cheap substitute for the real thing? And if she wanted him back, what then? What would he do if she took him back?

He jumped in the Cadillac and roared out of the strip mall in a cloud of exhaust. As he slipped into the traffic, the black Land Cruiser appeared behind him, bobbing and weaving through the traffic as it followed Ruffin's exhaust cloud out of the Chinese neighborhood toward Wilshire Boulevard. Ruffin had no idea he was being followed. He headed toward Polly's, a sandwich place near the city water department where Shanise worked, and looked for a parking place. He paid no more attention to the Land Cruiser than to any other SUV. That was the kind of car everybody seemed to be driving these days.

Strausser and Duvaloy watched through the windshield of the Land Cruiser. Strausser amused himself by snapping and unsnapping the cuffs of his western shirt. Both men looked annoyed, apprehensive, a little scared.

"Just one guy?" Strausser said. "Just one guy in the car?"

"It looks that way," Duvaloy said.

"Nobody else there?"

"Not that I can see."

"You better call," Strausser said.

"He said follow the car," Duvaloy said. "I followed the car."

"He said there'd be two guys."

"What the hell do you want me to do?"

"I think you better call. See what he wants us to do."

"Why don't you call him yourself if you're getting all wet about it?"

Frowning, Strausser pulled out his phone and dialed a number.

Inside Polly's, Ruffin brushed past the hostess and found Shanise at a small table, eating a tuna fish sandwich. At first she didn't seem to recognize him, but when she stood up she had tears in her eyes. She hugged him and he folded her warm body into his arms, bringing back memories he wasn't sure he wanted to have just then. She pulled back, like he'd held her a little too long. She couldn't help noticing his bandaged shoulder. "Kenny, I didn't recognize you at first," she said, smiling — the tears were gone, and she seemed nervous. "It's good to see you. It really is."

"You too."

"What's the matter with your shoulder? You get shot already?"

"It's nothing. Don't worry about it."

They sat down across from each other and she picked up her sandwich. "You want to order something?"

"No, that's okay."

"You mind if I go ahead and eat? I've got to get back."

"Sure, no problem."

"It's been a long time," she said. "You know I'm married now."

"I know. I heard that. You're still working for the city though. How you doing?"

"I'm fine."

"How's the boy? How's Jayden?"

She hesitated, looking down as she chewed on her sandwich. "He's just fine. He's a good boy. Almost a man."

"He's seventeen, right? Is he still in school?"

"He's still in school. Eleventh grade."

She pulled out her phone and showed him a picture of Jayden and herself with a man in a military uniform. They were posing like a happy family on a TV show. Ruffin knew he couldn't live up to this image of what a man was supposed to be like, even if he wanted to. Just seeing it made him angry, though he tried not to show it. The man had his arm around the boy. "That your husband?" he asked.

"That's Derek," she said, "when he was still in the Marines. He's raised Jayden, tried to show him how to stay focused, get the job done, stand up for himself without getting hurt. It hasn't been easy."

"I want to see him, Shanise."

The tears were back in her eyes. "Kenny, please leave him alone."

"He's my son."

"He don't know you. If he saw you he wouldn't know who you were, and you wouldn't know him. Derek don't want you to see him."

That was the wrong thing to say. Shanise knew that as soon as she said it.

"He ain't Derek's son," Ruffin said.

"Please just let him be. He's sort of crazy right now, trying out different things, being like different people, and one of them is you."

"I'm his father."

"Kenny" — she was pleading and he remembered what that was like, what it was like to be pissed off but unable to fight back because of the way she pleaded with her eyes — "you're a good man on the inside, I know that. But that's not the part of you he wants to be like. It's the part you show off on the street, the part he's heard people talk about, that he wants to be." She looked scared and that made Ruffin angry.

"Maybe that's who I am," he said.

"That's what Derek's afraid of."

"What you're afraid of too."

"No." Her eyes glistened back at him with the defiant hardness of lost love. "I know you better than that."

10

Morales and Burke sat in the front seat of their unmarked cruiser, watching the Chinese restaurant from the parking lot as they nibbled on burgers and fries they'd picked up at McDonalds. A few patrons came and went, but not the one they were watching for. The giant pudgy-faced waiter stepped out for a smoke and quickly ducked back inside. No sign of Ruffin, even though his appointment was at 1:00 o'clock and the cops had been there since 12:30.

"It's 1:30," Burke said. "We've been here over an hour. Either he's not coming or he's already left. We're wasting our time."

"Okay," Morales said. "Let's go inside and see if he's here."

"We're supposed to follow him, not meet him for lunch."

"What do you mean?"

"If he's in there, he's going to see us and know we're tailing him. Is that what you want?"

She opened the car door and stuck one foot outside. "I want to talk to him."

Burke didn't move. "Talk to him? What the hell about?"

"I'm not comfortable using him as a decoy," she said. "I want to see if I can convince him to work with us."

"Christ. We're just following him to see if he leads us to the shooters. Does that make him a decoy?"

"If they kill him before he kills them, then he was sort of a decoy, wasn't he? They already shot him once."

She climbed out and Burke followed her across the parking lot. "You know what, Morales?" Burke said. "Someday you're gonna get blown away by one of these scumbags you worry about so much."

Inside the restaurant Felipe stepped forward to welcome them, then backed away when he flashed their police badges. There was no sign of Ruffin or McGrath. As usual Chung sat heaped over his paperwork in the corner booth. When they stepped up to him he nodded but didn't offer to shake hands. They pulled up chairs and sat down.

"Where are your new parolees?" Morales asked.

"Ruffin and McGrath? They were in and out of here so fast I couldn't slow them down."

"What time did they get here?"

"I think it was a little before eleven."

Morales glared with frustration. "Didn't you get our phone message? You were supposed to call us if they got here early."

Chung's expression conveyed both an apology and, intentionally, the message that his apology was insincere. "I didn't have a chance," he said. "They blew in and out of here before I could call you. I can find them and put them on ice if you want."

"No," Morales said, "we don't want you to do that."

"We're following Ruffin around," Burke smirked, "hoping somebody will take another pop at him."

Morales frowned at Burke. "Did you get an address and phone number for Ruffin?" she asked Chung.

"He's staying at the shelter, isn't he?"

"No, he never showed up at the shelter. I thought you knew that."

Chung shrugged carelessly. "He seemed to think I'd cut him a break because he got shot getting off the bus."

"That asshole thinks the world owes him a living," Burke said.

"Getting shot doesn't give you any special status in this town," Chung nodded. "I tried to tell him that but he didn't seem to get it."

"He's lucky they sewed him back up," Burke agreed.

Morales said, "Somebody's trying to kill him."

"Sort of tears you up inside, don't it?" Burke said.

"Hey, if it gets him off the street," Chung shrugged. "Unless you want me to put him back in right now."

Morales didn't try to hide her contempt for this exchange, which was obviously intended to bait her. "Does he have any family in the area?" she asked.

Chung consulted a two-page parole report in one of his files. "His mother died when he was five. Raised by an aunt who is now deceased. No father, no brothers or sisters that we know of. He does have a son, address unknown. There must be an ex-wife or girlfriend somewhere."

She held out her hand. "Let me see that."

Parked across the street from Polly's, Strausser and Duvaloy kept watch in the Land Cruiser as a steady stream of trucks, buses, cars and motorcycles roared past them, backfiring and spewing exhaust into the smoggy air. "I'll be glad when that jerkoff comes out so we don't have to sit here anymore," Strausser said.

"What's the matter?" Duvaloy asked.

"The traffic noise is getting to me" Strausser said. He unsnapped his shirt cuffs, snapped them together, and unsnapped them again. He did this about ten times.

"Would you knock that off?" Duvaloy said. "It's annoying."

Strausser took out his Beretta and checked to make sure it was in working order. "This truck exhaust is getting to me too." He tapped his chest, stifling a cough. "I'm afraid it's gonna trigger an asthma attack."

"Put that away," Duvaloy said.

"I'm not taking any chances," Strausser said. "This guy's an animal."

Ruffin and Shanise came out of Polly's and stood near the curb, talking. Ruffin saw the Land Cruiser across the street but paid no attention to it. It meant nothing to him, just another SUV for rich people to ride around in.

"What are you going to do now, Kenny?" Shanise asked. "The same thing all over again?"

"Somebody took a shot at me before I was even off the bus," Ruffin said. "Killed a lady and almost killed her little girl standing next to me."

"What could you do about that?"

"Before I went inside, nobody would have done that. And if they did, they would've known what to expect. I had respect on the street and I knew how to keep it."

Shanise had that pleading look in her eyes again, but with an attitude — it wasn't just pleading, it was dissing him. "You call that respect?" she taunted. "People being afraid of you so don't kill them?"

"I never killed nobody."

A sharp explosion brought Ruffin's head spinning around and for a long instant he had a slow motion vision of death — slow enough that if there were bullets coming toward him he could have dodged them — but it was only a motorcycle backfiring. The motorcycle froze in space as the backfire exploded past him and then it sped away. He shot a glance up and down the street and saw nothing new, just the black Land Cruiser that had been there all along.

"You're lucky you went away," Shanise said. "At least you're still alive. All your so-called friends that you went to jail to keep from snitching on? They're all dead — OD'd, shot by gangs, shot by the cops. Nobody out there cares about you anymore."

"How come they're trying to kill me then?"

"Because that's the way your world works, Kenny. It's the only thing it knows how to do."

He turned away and stalked toward his car.

Shanise spent most of the afternoon at her desk in the water department fighting back the emotions her encounter with Ruffin had released. For seventeen years she'd dreaded the day he would come back, the opposite of how he must have felt looking forward to his release, and it didn't play out the way she'd imagined. He wasn't the angry, sullen kid who went inside, but a determined man who'd made peace with himself, if not with the world, yet a man who demanded respect, as he defined it. She'd married Derek mostly for Jayden's sake, hoping he'd keep him off the path his father took, and lately Derek had lost his grip, trying to be strict without showing Jayden any affection or any reason to respect him. Derek thought his exploits in the Marines earned him enough respect to last a lifetime, and maybe they did, but Jayden didn't think so. Ruffin was so much more impressive than Derek would ever be, and just for that reason she had to keep him away from Jayden until he got his life together. She didn't blame Ruffin for resenting Derek and wanting to make up for lost time with his son, but she couldn't let him see Jayden. And she realized now that Ruffin, all those years, had never been far from her own heart — she couldn't let him see that either.

11

Kimberly's place was more like a motel room than an apartment. Just a bedroom with a shag carpet, filled mostly by the bed, and a tiny bathroom. On the blotchy walls were pictures of seahorses and a view of the beach in Hawaii. In fact the one-story stucco building used to be a motel called the Wai Ki Ki and the whole place had a Hawaiian theme. In front there was an oblong pit filled with sand and weeds with a rusted sign warning visitors to swim at their own risk. The rug smelled like cat piss and the air conditioner put out more noise than air, but to McGrath, after eight years in the joint, the place was heaven on earth. There were no cops or prison guards in sight and if anybody got a blowjob it would be him and not some 280-pound Hell's Angel who'd backed him into a corner in the laundry.

In fact that item on his parole bucket list was the first to be checked off. Afterwards Kimberly lay beside him, sweating and gasping for breath. "I admire your work ethic, working girl," McGrath said. "Only hooker I ever knew who worked up a sweat."

"A day's work for a day's pay," she smiled. "Isn't that what made America great?"

He nodded, more out of patriotism than agreement, since hard work had never been part of his philosophy. In fact — apart from crime (which can be a bitch) and the jobs they gave him in the joint — he'd never done an honest day's work in his life, and he was proud of it. The work ethic was for suckers, although, with Kimberly wiping her lips beside him, he was too much of a gentleman to say so. "Me," he said, "I been a grifter all my life. Living by my wits. That's why them sons of bitches make me so mad. The money they're swindling me out of is what I planned to retire on. It's like robbing a man of his Social Security."

Kimberly stood up and padded toward the bathroom.

"The cops, the lawyers, the parole agents," he went on, "they're like a pack of wolves. They take a bite out of you every day until they chew you up. Then they spit you out."

"I guess that makes me one of them," she smirked, spitting loudly into the sink. She washed out her mouth and snapped the bathroom door shut behind her.

McGrath had to raise his voice to be heard over the running water. "I earned every penny of that money," he said. "Three full days of lying under oath. You think that ain't hard work?"

Inside the bathroom, Kimberly hunched over the sink with the water running as she whispered into her phone: "I'll keep him here as long as I can."

Morales and Burke had different philosophies when it came to police work. Burke's philosophy was the same as Hague's: Make an arrest as quickly as possible, expending the least amount of time and effort consistent with direction from above, then pass the suspect on to the D.A.'s office and the courts, to be indicted, arraigned, charged, tried, bargained with, convicted, sentenced, and handed off to Corrections, which would never correct him but only make him worse, leaving him eligible to repeat the process again and again until long after you were enjoying your retirement on some golf course in Arizona. Issues of guilt and innocence and correct legal procedure, which preoccupied the fake cops on TV, were not a problem in the real world. You knew who the criminals were, and for every crime they were innocent of there were a dozen others they were guilty of, so it didn't really matter which one they went to jail for. The procedures you followed to get them there didn't matter either, as long as they weren't the type of thing a slimy defense lawyer could take advantage of. Morales's philosophy was quaintly different. She still believed in the clichés she'd learned in ninth grade civics class at San Bernardino High School. Not being beaten into a confession, being innocent until proven guilty, having something resembling a fair trial — she still believed in all that crap. As far as Hague and Burke were concerned (and they talked about Morales all the time), she was a typical bleeding heart who should have been a social worker instead of a cop. It was an open secret that she'd been promoted to detective because she was a woman and a minority. She was a smart lady who worked a little too hard at being a hard worker, but she was out of her depth dealing with criminals, even though she seemed to care about them so much. One of these days, Burke and Hague agreed, she'd go down in flames. They only hoped she didn't take the whole department with her.

Back in the division station, Morales tried to use the information she got from Chung to draw a bead on Ruffin. No mother, no father, no brothers or sisters, just a son and an ex-wife or girlfriend somewhere. Morales pounded her keyboard for an hour searching the Department of Vital Statistics for the years just before and after Ruffin went to prison. Burke went out for coffee and came back and sat down at his desk, looking even more pissed off than usual.

"What's the matter?" Morales asked him.

"This coffee tastes like shit."

That was the issue of the day for Burke, and not for the first time.

"Listen to this," Morales said. "Ruffin's listed as the father of a boy named Jayden, born just after he went to prison. The mother's name is Shanise Robinson."

"Some whore. You'll never find her." Burke took a sip of his shitty coffee and threw the rest of it in the trash. "They need to do something about that vending machine."

"Why don't you go over to Starbucks?" Morales asked him. "I've heard they've got coffee over there."

"For three bucks," Burke said. "The hell with that." He tapped on his keyboard and squinted at his screen, reviewing a report on last night's Dodgers game.

Morales's keyboard clattered for another thirty minutes before she uncovered the next link. "I've got a current address," she said, "if it's the same person. There's a Shanise Robinson who works for the city water department."

"Why are you trying to find her?" Burke asked. "You think Ruffin'll go looking for the son?"

"I'm sure of it."

He stood up and peered over her shoulder, suddenly interested. "Okay, why don't we put a stake-out on the house, see if

Ruffin shows up? Follow this Shanise Robinson around for a few days. Maybe the shooters'll show up too."

"Isn't it bad enough that we're using Ruffin as a decoy?" Morales twisted around for a look into Burke's puffy, bloodshot eyes. "I'm not putting the mother's life in danger. Or the son's."

"You found her address easy enough," Burke said. "Whoever's gunning for Ruffin is probably over there already, waiting for him to show up."

"I guess you're right."

"Nothing we do is going to make it any worse."

It was hard to fault Burke's logic, but Morales still felt uncomfortable adding Ruffin's family to the list of decoys. She imagined herself talking to Shanise Robinson, warning her that Ruffin was back in town and might be bringing danger with him, not to set her up as a decoy but in fact trying to protect her and her son from whoever was stalking Ruffin. Maybe she could also get the point across that the police weren't the enemy, that they were doing this so Ruffin wouldn't land back in jail or die trying to protect his honor. At the very least she might be able to persuade Shanise — if she'd already been in touch with Ruffin — to give him a message for her. If she could talk to Ruffin — alone, without Burke muttering threats or insults in the background — maybe she could convince him that they ought to work together to find the shooters and bring them down.

Ruffin drove through the old neighborhood checking out what had changed in seventeen years and what hadn't. What had changed: More burned-out houses and boarded-up storefronts, some glitzy new Asian food joints with bars on the windows, cops marching four abreast in helmets and black body armor with dogs ahead of them straining on the leash. Some streets looked more like Juarez or Kabul than the L.A. he remembered, an occupied war zone where everybody had a secret plan to keep from getting killed by the cops or the gangbangers. What hadn't changed: junk cars, graffiti'd walls, crazy old women shouting at trucks as they passed, homeless guys scrounging through garbage cans, scary-eyed kids hanging around outside bars and liquor stores daring you to get out of your car so they can jump on you and steal whatever they can grab if you don't kick the shit out of them first. They weren't the same kids, though — they stared back at him and he didn't see anybody he recognized. When you're inside, he thought, there's no tomorrow, you settle into a timeless daze, but on the outside time rushes along, you can't get to the future soon enough, you burn yourself out like you're on crack, which you usually are. These aren't the same kids he used to see here — Shanise says they're all dead or in jail. This is a new generation who weren't even in school when you went inside and now here they are, thinking about killing you. He could see it in their eyes.

He parked in front of a ramshackle daycare center with a sign that read "Kids Paradise." An elderly lady named Lucille hovered over the sidewalk with a broom.

"Hey, Lucille," he said, slipping out of the car. "How you doing?"

"Kenny? Is that you?"

He hugged her and she hugged him back. Her head came to the middle of his chest. She remembered him from when he came up that high on her. Neither of them noticed the black Land Cruiser that stopped along the curb half a block away.

"I heard you was out," Lucille said.

"Yeah, I'm out. Trying to get my life back together."

She took a step back to get a look at him. "You look good," she said. "Considering."

He had to smile. "So do you," he said. "Considering."

She laughed. "I'm a little older, that's all." She took a half-hearted swipe at the sidewalk with her broom, and asked: "You seen Jayden yet?"

"Not yet. Shanise is trying to keep me away from him."

"She don't want the boy to get hurt."

"I know that," Ruffin said. "Somebody tried to kill me already."

"I heard about that too."

That didn't surprise Ruffin. Lucille knew everything that went on in the neighborhood, she knew about the kids, the ministers, the politicians, the cops. Even the criminals — she knew everything there was to know about the criminals.

"Got any idea who it was?" Ruffin asked her.

"You ain't gonna go after him?"

He shrugged and smiled a little, to show what a minor thing that would be. "Maybe just scare him a little."

"I heard it was a kid named Alonzo Payne," she said. "I call him a kid because that's how I remember him, but he ain't no kid anymore. Must be twenty-one, twenty-two by now. Hangs out with his gang in front of that Wellington's crab place on East Washington."

"Who does he work for?"

She shrugged. "I doubt if anybody would hire him, even for shooting somebody."

"Think I'll go get me some crabs," Ruffin said.

"Kenny, promise me you'll be careful." She reached out and squeezed his hand. "That man'll kill you."

12

Morales had decided, without mentioning it to Burke, to pay a surprise visit to Shanise Robinson that night on her way home from work. Burke would have scoffed at the notion of minding the public's business when he could be home drinking beer and watching a ball game, but Morales viewed her job as a 24/7 commitment. The last thing she wanted to do was put Shanise Robinson or her son in danger, but (as Burke pointed out) that was probably already the case if she was the right person and the shooters were as determined to find Ruffin as Morales was. The woman hadn't been that hard to find.

It was 4:00 o'clock, too early to go looking for Shanise, who worked at the water department. She probably wouldn't be home from work for a couple of hours. To pass the time, Morales shifted the focus of her internet search from Ruffin to the man he'd last been seen with: Cat McGrath. If they couldn't find one of the cons, why not look for the other?

Both Burke and Hague seemed to regard McGrath as a harmless buffoon. The archives of the *L.A. Times* told a different story. "Here's some stuff about the racket McGrath was sent up for," she told Burke. "They brought in underage girls from a Chinese freighter docked in Long Beach and trucked them around to parties at some of the big hotels."

"Yeah, I sort of remember that," Burke said as he typed into his computer.

"McGrath was the one who brought the girl who was strangled to the Russian's hotel room."

"Yeah," Burke laughed. "He copped a plea and then pissed off the judge so much she put him away for ten years. That jackass can't keep his gob shut."

"They never found the Russian, did they?"

Burke didn't answer and Morales became aware of someone standing behind her. The stale cigarette smell told her it was Hague, who spent half his day migrating back and forth to the men's room to smoke. He leaned on the back of her chair peering over her shoulder at the screen. "Morales," he said, "I told you to leave that ancient history alone."

She twisted around to face him. "There's something about McGrath—"

"You people have a hard time following orders, don't you? This isn't a piñata party."

"A piñata party?" Morales couldn't believe what he just said.

"Just joking," Hague said. "Lighten up."

"I'm investigating the case you assigned me to." She glanced at Burke, who rolled his eyes toward the ceiling.

"I'm taking you off the shooting case," Hague said.

"What do you mean?"

"Since you're so interested in whores, I'm thinking we ought to put you in Vice for a couple of months."

"They weren't whores. They were 14-year-old girls who thought they were going—"

"The only girl I care about," he interrupted, "is the one the Commissioner keeps calling me about. The one who got shot getting off that bus. He's a very caring man, the Commissioner, and when he cares about something you damn well better care about it too."

Ruffin drove around the block a couple times checking out Wellington's bar where Lucille said he'd find Alonzo. It was a quiet place at that time of day, the door standing open next to a service window that advertised "Fresh Crabs." Some gang-banger wannabes in basketball shorts down to their ankles huddled around the door trying to look more than twelve years old. Ruffin didn't see Alonzo but he thought he recognized the kid named Earl from the night before. He climbed out of the car, swinging the tire iron, and walked toward the door. The kids stopped talking when they saw him. Most of them melted out of sight. By the time he reached the door only two were left: Earl and a younger kid named Shane with a crazed eye that said he didn't expect to be on the planet much longer.

Earl stepped in front of the door. "This a crab place," he said. "Ain't no flat tires here."

"Some of them crawdads got shells that need cracking," Ruffin said, hefting the tire iron.

"You looking for Alonzo, he ain't here."

"I say he is," Ruffin said.

"I say he ain't."

It was that kind of debate. Not a lot of give and take or supporting evidence on either side. It might have gone on forever if Ruffin didn't cut to the chase. "Only one way to find out," he said. He punched Earl in the stomach, doubling him over, then swung the tire iron at Shane, knocking him back into the wall. Earl jumped on him from behind. Ruffin pulled

him down by the hair and kicked him in the back, then pounded his neck with his fists. When both of the punks were down
he took their guns and stuck them in his pockets. They whimpered on the sidewalk with their arms wrapped over their
heads as if they thought their tattoos could stop bullets.

Ruffin strode through the door and the bar room clatter
stopped. A baseball game flickered on the TV over the bar —
the Dodgers were losing to the Cubs in Chicago — but by the
time he sat down the room had emptied out and there was
nobody to watch it. When he laid his tire iron in front of him
on the bar, the bartender pretended not to notice it. He was
one of those sad-eyed bartenders who look like they've seen
everything and probably have. "Get you something?" he asked.

"A beer and some crab legs," Ruffin said. "Hottest kind
you got, with a bowl of cayenne on the side."

The bartender brought him a bottle of Coors. Then he
scooped out a platter of hot crab legs and laid them front of
him, along with a large bowl of red cayenne pepper. "You the
guy they sent over to clean out the men's room?" he asked.

"Something in there need cleaning out?"

"Uh-huh. Something real bad's going on in there that needs
cleaning out. Be careful, though. Wouldn't want anybody to
get hurt."

Ruffin hooked the tire iron under his belt, picked up the
bowl of cayenne, and headed for the men's room.

Kimberly slipped out of the bathroom and nestled back in
bed with McGrath. She needed to stall for time and there was
only one sure way to do it, revolting as it was. "I won't charge

extra if you want an instant replay," she said, twirling her finger down his chest.

"See, that's the difference between you and me, Kimberly," McGrath said. "When I do a job I expect to get paid. I don't like being used."

"This is a hooker you're talking to," she reminded him.

"Hell, I ain't using you. You're getting paid for what you do."

She rolled over and started kissing him, though not on the lips. A hooker, he'd learned, would do anything you wanted her to do except kiss you on the lips. It was like she was saving that for marriage. He didn't mind as long as she kissed him everywhere else. "Your friend Kenny," she said, working her way down, "what's he like?"

"Ruffin's one bad hombre," McGrath said, watching her as best he could. "Goes around with guns, knives, razor blades in all his pockets. Keeps a tire iron under the front seat of the car. Pass that on to the boss. He don't want to mess with Ruffin."

"What boss are you talking about?"

"Chung's uncle. That's who you work for, ain't it?"

"I've never met that guy," she said, rolling her big brown eyes up to look at him. He liked it when they looked up at him.

"You work for Chung, then?"

"Until I'm off parole."

"What do you hear about the uncle?" McGrath asked.

"A few years back there was this Chinese girl" — Kimberly rolled backwards and raised her head for a better look — "Hey, now I know who you are! You're the scumbag who took that girl to the Russian's hotel room. I saw your picture on TV."

McGrath tried to reassure her. "Now, don't go getting the wrong idea," he said. "I had no way of knowing what was gonna happen to that girl. I thought she was applying to secretarial school."

"Did you strangle her?"

"Hell, no, but I know who did, and it warn't no Russian."

"Who was it then?"

"That's private information," McGrath said with a smirk, "and I plan on taking it to the bank. You play your cards right, you can go there with me."

Ruffin burst into the men's room at Wellington's and kicked open the stall. Alonzo sat on the closed toilet seat, nodding off with a syringe in his arm. He scrambled to stand up but Ruffin grabbed him and threw the cayenne pepper in his eyes. He screamed, trying to cover his face.

"Here, let me wash that off for you." Ruffin wrapped his hands around Alonzo's throat and turned him over and stuck his head into the toilet bowl and flushed it, then pulled him out, sputtering. "That's how a piece of shit feels. But you knew that already, didn't you?"

"I'll kill you!"

Ruffin ran his hands over Alonzo to make sure he didn't have a gun on him. "Listen to me," Ruffin said. "I been seeing a little too much of you lately. Next time I see you's gonna be the last time."

"Ain't gonna be a next time. You'll be a dead man long before that."

There was no sign of the bartender or anybody else when
Ruffin strolled back through the bar. It was the top of the
ninth inning and nobody was there to watch the Dodgers lose.
Alonzo's gang had disappeared. Ruffin climbed back in the
Cadillac and cruised away.

The Toyota Land Cruiser followed at a distance.

13

It was the first time Ruffin ever heard a phone ringing in a car. The damn thing was in his pocket and made him jump with fright when it rang. By the time he could stop the car and answer it, the call was gone.

The phone rang again and this time Ruffin answered it in time to hear McGrath's twangy voice saying, "What's the matter? You in the middle of somebody?"

"Just couldn't figure out how to answer this damn phone," Ruffin said.

"Can you come pick me up?" McGrath had slipped out of Kimberly's apartment and walked a couple blocks to a Seven Eleven. She begged him to stay — that's the way women were, they just couldn't get enough of him — but he'd accomplished what he wanted to accomplish and it was time to move on. "Florence and San Pedro," he told Ruffin. "In front of the Seven Eleven."

"Give me a half hour," Ruffin said. He'd driven into an industrial zone and needed to make a stop before he picked up McGrath. On a deserted street he parked next to a vacant lot overgrown with weeds and pulled out the two guns he'd taken from Alonzo's bodyguards. They were nice pieces, 45-caliber Glock 21's, probably like the one Alonzo'd shot him with the night before. He hefted them in his hand, just to remember what it was like to hold a gun. It was like touching a woman, something you don't forget no matter how long they keep you locked up, and it gave him the same kind of thrill, a feeling of manhood and confidence and danger because you never knew what would happen when you held a gun or touched a woman. But then he remembered what McGrath had said about being caught with a gun. That was a sure ticket back to San Quentin where he'd have no manhood or confidence but only the deadly thrill of staying alive for another day. No point carrying a piece until he needed it — he could always get one then. He emptied the bullets down a storm drain and tossed the two Glocks into the weeds in the middle of the vacant lot. The last thing he wanted was to leave those guns lying around where some kid like Jayden might find them.

Alonzo lived in a shabby rented house with a wide front porch which was also his business headquarters. That evening he met with his team (he never called them his gang) on the front porch. They sat on the railing across from him, their backs to the street. Alonzo was often angry and abusive to the team — he worked himself into a frenzy if somebody didn't do what he was told — but that night the team noticed something different about him: a wild, raging look in his eyes. In fact his eyes were red and inflamed from the cayenne pepper Ruffin had thrown in them, but he didn't tell them about that. What happened in the Wellington's men's room would never be mentioned, and if anybody found out about it they wouldn't be breathing for long.

"You all know how it went down at the hospital last night," Alonzo said. "That mother do a job on DeWayne big time, kick him in the head, then today he show up at Wellington's like he own the place. Earl and Shane seen him there. When he come inside I whup his ass and chase him out of there like a dog. He don't lay a hand on me or I woulda wasted him."

The team murmured its shock and disapproval:

"Do a job on DeWayne."

"Kick him in the head."

"Big time."

"In the hood?"

"Shit."

"I'm talking to y'all so shut up," Alonzo said. "What I'm telling you is we ain't gonna put up with that shit. The man's going down. You hear me? He's going down all the way."

The team nodded, a little less enthusiastically:

"Man's going down."

"All the way."

"Ain't gonna put up with that shit."

Alonzo stamped his foot on the wooden porch to get their attention. "One of you pussies gonna do it, hear?" he yelled. "One of you pussies gonna take out his ass."

The team faced him in stony silence.

"Maybe you all didn't hear me," Alonzo shouted, his eyes even redder than before. "Maybe you all deaf. So I'm telling you loud and clear: If somebody don't off that son of a bitch by tomorrow I'm gonna shoot every one of you pussies' asses before I shoot his."

He pivoted and stalked into the house. As the team drifted away from the porch, somebody watching from the street — if anybody'd dared to watch Alonzo's house from the street — would have noticed Earl and Shane slinking away with their eyes cast down.

And Jayden a few steps behind them, looking troubled, anxious, and scared.

Morales left work early and drove around aimlessly, distracted by the angry scenarios cycling through her mind. She imagined disobeying Hague to find the scumbags who shot Luisa Salazar, even though he'd taken her off the case. Disobeying Hague to rescue teenage prostitutes in Chinatown. Telling Hague to take this job and shove it. Telling the Commissioner to take this job and shove it. Filing a discrimination complaint against Hague, the Commissioner, the department and the whole damn city — no, that would only make her look weak. Better yet: kicking Hague in the balls, kicking the Commissioner in the balls, and while she was at it kicking Burke in the balls for being such a spineless sack of shit who'd never stand up to Hague or anybody else in spite of his bad cop machismo act. Then she did something she never did: she stopped at a bar and had a drink — actually a few drinks — which only inflamed her imagination further. The bar was called Antonito's and it was a great place to think about the mayhem she'd like to inflict on the men who wanted to lord it over her. Did she have trouble following orders? Did she think life was a piñata party? There was nothing she wouldn't do to get Hague back for that remark and for taking her off the case. But why couldn't she just ignore him? Why couldn't she, in her own mind, refuse to be reassigned? Keep doing exactly what she'd been doing: link up with Ruffin to find the shooters before they found him, do everything in her power to stop the bloodbath that would surely occur unless she could use the power of the law against the forces of chaos and destruction? What a crock of shit. How many drinks had she had anyway? Did she seriously think Ruffin would do the right thing? He was a criminal, two days out of San Quentin. Still there was something genuine about him that made her feel — in her current state — that he had some good in him. Was she just fooling herself?

The bar was full of men — handsome men, ugly men, black men, white men, fat men, thin men — but none of them paid any attention to Morales. Did she look like a cop? she wondered. Or was it because they could tell how angry she was?

14

Ruffin picked up McGrath in front of the Seven Eleven at Florence and San Pedro and they cruised down Florence in a law-abiding fashion with Ruffin at the wheel until McGrath turned the radio to a jangly country music station. "I can't stand this shit," Ruffin said. He reached over and fiddled with the radio until he found some R&B.

McGrath waited about ten seconds and tuned it back to the country station. "I heard enough of that shit in the joint to last me the rest of my life."

Ruffin switched it back to R&B. "Which ain't gonna be very long if you touch that dial again."

McGrath curled his hand over the dial. "How you gonna carry out that threat when you're driving?"

Ruffin knew McGrath never wore a seat belt. He slammed on the brakes and McGrath came an inch away from smashing his beautiful prison teeth on the dashboard. He was pissed but for once he held his tongue, probably feeling lucky he didn't bite it off. He consoled himself with a slug of Wild Turkey.

"I'm driving," Ruffin said, "so I tune the radio."

"The hell you do," McGrath said. He reached over and snapped it off. More Wild Turkey.

Ruffin welcomed the silence but knew it couldn't last.

"How was it seeing Shanise?" McGrath asked him.

"Sort of frustrating," Ruffin said. "I guess I forgot what women are like."

"Yeah, that always comes as a shock after being in the joint."

"She's got a husband now," Ruffin said. "An ex-Marine, who won't let me see my son."

"That's harsh," McGrath said. "I mean, you ain't exactly a Eagle scout or a war hero. Matter of fact, with all due respect, what you are is a career criminal who just got out of San Quentin after sixteen years—"

"Seventeen."

"Seventeen, excuse me — but he's got no right to interfere with your relationship with your son. That's sacrosanct."

"You're damn right it is."

"Even if he is a ex-Marine who could kick your ass to kingdom come and back again."

"Worst part is," Ruffin said, "Shanise is on his side."

McGrath laughed out loud. "I gotta hand it to you, Ruffin," he said. "Everybody's got his enemies — cops, gangsters, girlfriends, jealous husbands — but you got all of them at once. It's like your enemy is the world itself."

They turned onto Alameda and headed toward downtown. "How was your date with Kimberly?" Ruffin asked.

"It's been a while since I been with a woman," McGrath said, "so I probably shouldn't criticize. All I can say is, a dollar sure don't go as far as it used to."

A huge neon sign in the shape of a naked woman — "Suzy's Gentlemen's Club" — beckoned them into a parking lot filled with jeeps and pickup trucks. "Speaking of the Almighty Dollar," McGrath said, "let's pull in here. I wonder if the strippers still take singles."

Strausser and Duvaloy found it easy to keep the smoke-belching Cadillac in their sights. They stayed half a block behind and made sure the Land Cruiser blended into the traffic. While Strausser drove, Duvaloy held his phone to his ear. "We finally got both of them together," he said into the phone. "Swerving down East Olympic in an old green Cadillac. It looks like they're stopping at a strip club."

The Cadillac lurched into the parking lot of Suzy's Gentlemen's Club. Strausser kept going and Duvaloy tried to keep his eye on the Cadillac as they circled into a gas station to turn around.

"They're going inside," Duvaloy said into the phone. "Suzy's Gentlemen's Club. You got any connections at this place? Somebody you could call who could flush them out of there for us? We'll take it from there."

Duvaloy grinned as he heard the response. "Okay," he said. "You do that. We'll wait for them outside."

Two young bouncers, one white, the other black, guarded the entrance to Suzy's, checking ID's and welcoming the customers with menacing looks. Ruffin and McGrath barged past them without slowing down or making eye contact. They weren't about to take any shit from those pissants. The hostess spotted them as recent parolees as soon as they walked through the door. Parolees are like kids in a candy store, she always said, stumbling in with saucer eyes and twitchy fingers, their gate money burning holes in their pockets. Sycamore — that was the hostess's name — greeted the new arrivals warmly, escorted them to the big circular bar, and motioned to the topless bartender for a free round of drinks. Bass-heavy porno music pounded around them like a sex-crazed heartbeat.

Ruffin and McGrath chased a few shots down with a few beers. Exotic dancers of all races, creeds and colors and from all corners of the globe frolicked above them on shiny metal poles to the throb of the porno music. It was like Breast Awareness Week at the UN General Assembly. They thought they'd died and gone to heaven.

"You two gentlemen sit down right here and I'll send a couple of gals over to keep you company," Sycamore said in her soft Southern drawl. "How do you like 'em? Rare, medium or well done?"

"Black on the outside, pink in the middle for me," Ruffin said. He jerked his thumb toward McGrath: "Shriveled up with lots of tattoos for him."

"And bald," McGrath said, thinking it was a joke. "Don't forget bald."

Sycamore came back leading three women: a black one and a white one for Ruffin, and — true to Ruffin's specifications — a shriveled up Asian with lots of tattoos for McGrath. Her tattoos weren't like McGrath's — more manga than Aryan Brotherhood — and she had enough piercings in her face for a long weekend of bass fishing. She wasn't exactly bald: she had a skinny rat tail that started on the top of her head and hung halfway down her back. If she was topless (Ruffin couldn't recall that detail later), it wasn't anything that stuck in your mind.

"Be careful what you wish for," Ruffin told McGrath.

"It's you that wished this on me, you son of a bitch."

The woman's name was Tamarind. "Is what you want a private dance?" she asked earnestly.

"Well, that depends," McGrath said, quoting his favorite statesman, "on what the meaning of 'is' is. If 'is' means that is what I want, then I don't want it. If it means that ain't what I want, then I want it. Understand?"

Tamarind pouted when she realized he was making fun of her.

"Oh, hell," McGrath said, "that's a cute little pout you got there. I think we can do business together." He hooked his arm around her elbow and escorted her away.

The other two women pawed at Ruffin from either side, enticing him with their eyes and their high-tech breasts. "What's your name?" he asked the white one.

"Tango," she said. "That's a dance."

"I'm Vixen," the black one said. "That's a fox."

"I thought Vixen was one of Santa's reindeer," the white girl said. "On Dasher, on Dancer and Prancer—"

"I wouldn't know about that," Vixen cut her off. "I'm Jewish."

Tango and Vixen were topless and sexy but all this stupid chatter by strippers with fake breasts and fake names was turning Ruffin off. He'd dreamed about women every night for seventeen years but the ones he dreamed about weren't like this. Sometimes they looked like Shanise but most of the time they weren't even women he'd actually known, they were phantoms, very detailed and realistic phantoms created by his own imagination or some deeper force within him, a reflection of a past or future life or maybe a life lived by someone else. He felt a powerful arousal taking him over but even as it did, he grew aware of an equal force pulling him in the opposite direction, the assertion of his freedom to choose what he would do. This was his first day of freedom and he resisted falling into any kind of entrapment, even by the instincts he'd fought to preserve in his captivity.

Sycamore materialized in front of him, smiling at the women in his arms. "How about some drinks for these girls?" she asked Ruffin. "They're thirsty." She signaled to the bartender who brought a round of watery drinks that Ruffin had to pay for. Then the hostess whispered something in Vixen's ear and glided away.

"C'mon, baby," Vixen said, tugging on his arm. "How about a date?"

Tango stroked his neck, his chest, his thigh. The two of them snuggled against him and lightly kissed his cheeks. He could feel their lips, their breath, their hair trailing down onto his neck.

"A date for three?" he said.

"Why not?" they both said. Then they laughed because they'd both said the same thing.

"Where did McGrath go with that Chinese girl?" he asked.

"She ain't Chinese," Vixen said.

"She's from North Korea," Tango explained.

"I don't care where she's from. Where'd she take him? You got some kind of back room here?"

"Come on, we'll show you."

Vixen took his hand and pulled him around the bar, Tango jiggling along beside him. He felt that he had surrendered to their superior power. Past the stage with its strobing lights and twirling strippers, weaving between low tables filled with smirking truckers and gawking businessmen, dodging cocktail waitresses hoisting trays of drinks, they led him through a bead curtain down a dark corridor, then through a heavy door into a shadowy room furnished with low plush couches and flat-screen TVs running porno loops on the walls. A door opened on the other end and McGrath came in with Tamarind behind him, both of them prodded forward by the two bouncers Ruffin had seen at the front door, brandishing sawed-off pool cues. McGrath looked a little sick, like he'd just had a narrow escape.

The bouncers clicked the door shut behind them and stood facing Ruffin with their pool cues raised. Tango and Vixen melted into the shadows behind Tamarind.

"The party's over," one of the bouncers said. He was a well-built black guy though not as big as Ruffin. About twenty-five and his face was clear and unscarred — either he was a Kung Fu master, Ruffin thought, or he'd never been in a real fight. The other guy was milky white with blond hair and a fat lower lip that made look stupid. Likewise, not a scar or even a tattoo in sight. Never been in a fight and never been in jail.

"What's this bullshit?" Ruffin asked. He wished he'd kept the Glocks he took from Alonzo's gang. Had he walked into a trap?

McGrath spoke up before the bouncers could react. "This goes way beyond bullshit, Ruffin," he said. Ruffin saw a glint of defiance, even superiority, in his eyes, like he thought he could outsmart these two young punks.

"Horseshit, then," Ruffin said, playing along.

"No," McGrath corrected him, "it ain't horseshit neither. This is on a whole 'nother level than horseshit."

"Pigshit?"

"Much bigger than pigshit."

"Chickenshit?" the stupid-looking bouncer ventured.

"That's a good guess, coming from a pissant like you. You must know just about everything there is to know about chickenshit."

The black bouncer stepped forward but McGrath waved him off. "But it still ain't the right answer," he said, playing on their curiosity. "Dogshit is what it is. A steaming pile of dogshit like you see the rich bitches in Santa Monica picking up off the beach in little plastic bags. What do they do with it when they get it home? That's what I'd like to know."

"All right, cut the shit!" the black bouncer yelled. "It's time for you two assholes to get the hell out of here."

"Y'all had best leave," the white bouncer agreed. He sounded like a politician from Louisiana or East Texas.

"I don't get this," Ruffin said. "Why are you throwing us out?"

"It don't matter why we're throwing you out," the black bouncer said. "We're the bouncers. That's what we do. We throw people out when they ain't wanted here anymore." He pointed to the door that led into the bar. "You're going through that door and then out through the front entrance where you came in. That's what you're gonna do. Right now."

Ruffin felt a rush of alarm, the way you feel in the joint when you step into the yard and you know there's going to be a fight. They'd been set up. Somebody was waiting for them outside the front entrance. If they did what the bouncers said, they wouldn't make it back to the car alive.

"You know, Ruffin," McGrath said, "when I get in a situation like this, the thing I always ask myself is: What would Jesus do?"

"Amen," the stupid white bouncer nodded.

"Didn't he say turn the other cheek?" Ruffin asked.

"He did," McGrath allowed. "He said that on one occasion. But in this case I think he'd say something different. I think he'd say: Go ahead and kick their ass!"

Ruffin knew McGrath well enough by this time to expect something like this, and he was ready for it. Even before the words were out of McGrath's mouth he leaped on the white bouncer, grabbed his pool cue and smashed the black one over the head with it, making sure he left a deep gash on his cheek. Then he turned back to the white one and gave him the same treatment. McGrath did his part by kicking both of them when they were down. They ended up moaning on the floor, barely conscious, trying to protect their faces. Tamarind sobbed by herself on one of the couches.

Tango and Vixen were all over Ruffin again. "You're our hero," Vixen said, nibbling on his ear lobe. "Those bouncers are a couple of douche bags."

"College students on work-study," Tango explained.

"Summer interns, actually."

"That's what we are too."

"What college is that?" McGrath demanded. "That's where I want to go after I get my GED."

Vixen eyed him up and down. "I doubt if you'd pass the entrance exam."

"Sorry to disappoint you, ladies," Ruffin said, peeling himself away from them, "but we got to get our asses out of here. Could you do me a favor? Go out front and see if anybody's watching the entrance — especially if they're pointing guns at it — and do everything you can to grab their attention."

"Oh, we know how to do that," Tango smiled.

"Keep them occupied for a little while, if you know what I mean."

"Yeah, we can do that, can't we, Vixen?"

Ruffin thanked them with a smile and ducked out the rear exit with McGrath. Vixen and Tango put on their halter tops and hurried through the bar and out the front entrance. Strausser and Duvaloy weren't hard to spot in the Land Cruiser, watching the entrance with their Berettas on their laps. The strippers danced up to the Land Cruiser and crawled in on top of them.

By this time Ruffin and McGrath had slipped out the back exit. They circled the parking lot, jumped into the Cadillac and were cruising down East Olympic before Tango and Vixen came up for air.

15

Morales slipped out of Antonito's without a passing glance from any of the men at the bar. Two blocks away, she sat in her Ford Focus sobering up as she thought about the Luisa Salazar case, which she couldn't get out of her mind. Talking to Ruffin would definitely be looking for trouble but she was going to do it anyway. If he didn't know who the shooters were, he was bound to find out soon enough. And then what? A few dead bodies would turn up in some alley and that would be the end of it. Somebody would go after Ruffin for revenge and the cycle of violence would continue. For Luisa Salazar there'd be no justice, no closure — unless she died: then she'd get the kind of closure her mother got, the closure of being dead and forgotten in a cold case file. Why did it matter? Morales asked herself. Why couldn't she be like Burke and just let the law of the jungle take its course? Murders in the city were up a thousand percent but nine tenths of them were killers killing other killers before they killed them. Why risk your own life trying to stop this insanity?

Morales sat there a while longer, then drove off to look for Shanise Robinson's house. It wasn't hard to find: a tidy bungalow in a lower middle class neighborhood, which in L.A. means it probably cost a million dollars in Monopoly money borrowed from an insolvent bank. Morales parked on a side street with a view of the house. Maybe Ruffin would show up, she thought; maybe the shooters would be there to greet him. In that event she might be able to head off a disaster. If nobody showed up by the time it got dark, she'd knock on the door and try to talk to Shanise. She rolled up her windows and started the engine so she could keep them from steaming up. The air was close: dark clouds were gathering into thunderstorms. The weather station said it was going to be a bad night.

Ruffin saw lightning flash over the ocean and the mountains north along the coast. When the rain started, it came down in sheets, which made driving difficult. The wipers scuttled across the windshield in a desperate clatter. He kept his eye on the rear-view mirror. "That SUV the strippers jumped in give me a bad feeling," he told McGrath.

"Could that be because the guys in it were planning to kill us?" McGrath asked.

Ruffin had noticed the Land Cruiser behind him when he left Wellington's, but he'd paid no attention to it. Now, thinking back, he remembered seeing an SUV like that across from Polly's and down the street from Lucille's pre-school. Whoever it was had been tailing him all day. At least it wasn't Alonzo and his gang – they'd been hanging out at Wellington's — but didn't that make it worse? Two separate gangs trying to kill him before he'd been back in L.A. for 24 hours?

"The guys in it were white," he told McGrath.

"You're an equal opportunity assassination target," McGrath laughed. "I'll give you credit for that."

A lightning bolt made the world stand still, waiting for the thunder. Ruffin turned off East Olympic and headed south on San Pedro. "How'd you like that Tamarind?" he asked McGrath.

"Couldn't get past the hardware," McGrath said.

"Those piercings sort of turn you off?"

McGrath gazed out at the rain and shook his head. "All I can say is, you don't want a blowjob from that bitch during an electrical storm."

Shanise and Derek stood in the kitchen cleaning up after dinner when someone knocked on the front door. The dinner hadn't been a pleasant one, with Derek and Jayden at each other's throats as usual. Derek was still fuming over some of the things Jayden had said. Jayden had stomped upstairs. Shanise walked through the living room and peeked through the eyehole before opening the door. It was a woman — by herself, white, maybe Hispanic. She wore plain clothes but she looked like a cop. That made Shanise feel a little queasy. She opened the door and the woman held up an LAPD badge.

"Ms. Robinson?" she said. "Detective Julie Morales, LAPD. Mind if I come in?"

Shanise hesitated before letting her come in out of the rain. Once they're in your house you're fair game, she'd been told. They don't need a warrant after you let them in. They don't even have to give you a Miranda warning before they question you. Shanise didn't want this cop talking to Jayden, or even to Derek. "What's this about?" she asked.

"It's about Kenny Ruffin," Morales said. "Does that name mean anything to you?"

"It might."

"He was released from prison a couple of days ago."

"I didn't know that." The cop didn't believe her but she didn't care: the lie was for Derek's benefit. Woman to woman, that was something Morales could understand without being told.

"He hasn't tried to contact you?" Morales asked.

"I doubt if he will."

"May I come in? It's pouring out here."

"I don't allow guns in my house."

"I'm not armed."

Shanise stood back as Morales stepped on the little rug inside the door. It was barely big enough to hold her, but Shanise wasn't going to let her come any farther. "Is there some problem?" she asked. "Is he in trouble already?"

"He's not in any trouble with the police," Morales said. "But somebody took a shot at him the minute he stepped off the bus from San Quentin and then went after him at the emergency room. Probably some of his old friends welcoming him back."

"I'm not surprised," Shanise said.

"You have any idea who it might have been?"

Shanise shook her head.

"Whoever it was might come over here looking for him," Morales said. "It was easy for me to find you so it would be just as easy for them. I thought you ought to know that."

"Thanks."

"Probably nothing will happen. But anyway I wanted to let you know that Ruffin's back in L.A. If he makes any unwanted contact with you or your son, please give me a call."

"How do you know anything about my son?" Shanise bristled.

"Public records." Morales made it sound routine but Shanise knew it wasn't routine. She worked for the water department where everything was public records, and nobody knew what was in them unless they spent hours searching through them. Her hand started to tremble at the mention of her son. She'd been so worried about Jayden lately, so afraid she'd turn on the TV and see his picture, the latest casualty in the drug wars or shot by the police. Derek tried to keep Jayden on the straight and narrow but that only made things worse. It was months since she'd been able to sleep.

"Okay," Shanise said, hoping the cop would leave if she agreed with her. "I'll let you know. But I don't expect to hear from him."

"If you do talk to him," Morales said, "please ask him to call me." She handed Shanise one of her cards. "Just give him my number and ask him to call me as soon as he can, okay? It's important, for his own protection. He's not in any trouble with the police."

Shanise looked worried. "Okay."

"And if anybody comes around looking for him, call me right away."

Shanise closed the door behind Morales and turned to find Derek glaring at her from the kitchen. "You talked to him, didn't you?" he said.

"He called me. He wants to see Jayden."

Derek frowned and shook his head. "That's not going to happen."

Jayden had come down the stairs into the living room. "What was that cop doing here?"

"What's the matter?" Derek asked. "Afraid she was looking for you or one of your scummy friends?"

Jayden lurched toward Derek as if he was going to punch him, but he stopped about ten feet away. "You don't know anything about me or my friends," he said.

"I'll tell you one thing I know," Derek said. "You keep on the way you're going, pretty soon you're going to end up like your famous dad. Is that who you want to be?"

"People respected him," Jayden said. "They still do. Nobody respects you."

"Jayden," Shanise said, "I don't want to hear—"

"Go ahead," Derek said. "See if you can pick up where he left off. I doubt if you've got the cojones. In the Marines we had a word for guys like you."

Shanise was in tears. "Derek, stop it!"

Jayden turned around and stormed out the front door.

16

Shanise waited until Derek went out to move his pickup into the garage before she dialed Ruffin's number. He and McGrath were sitting in the takeout line at McDonalds, McGrath behind the wheel, trying to make up their minds what to order. Ruffin heard his phone buzz and answered it.

"Kenny, can you talk?" Shanise said.

"Sure, I can talk."

"This woman cop came to my house, said her name was Morales."

Ruffin didn't like it that Morales had gone looking for Shanise. "What was she doing there?"

"She's looking for you, says it's important. I told her I didn't know you were back."

"What'd she want?"

"She said she needs to talk to you. You're not in any trouble with the cops, she said. But call her—it's important, soon as possible. You want her number?"

"I already got it." Now that he had Shanise on the phone he had to ask her again: "When am I gonna be able to see Jayden?"

"We can't talk about that now. I've got to get off the phone."

"That bitch jacking you around again?" McGrath asked when Ruffin hung up.

"Shut up."

Ruffin called in his order — bacon cheeseburger, large fries—and left McGrath in the takeout line and ran through the rain into the restaurant so he could call Morales without McGrath listening. "Why'd you go to Shanise's house?" he asked Morales. "How'd you know where to find her?"

"I'm a cop," Morales said. "I can find people."

"Leave her alone."

"I was hoping she could help me find you."

"She did," Ruffin said. "You find them shooters yet?"

"No. Have you?"

"Not yet."

"That's why I've got to talk to you. I think we can help each other." Morales asked him to meet her for a drink at a brew pub in Santa Monica.

"You gonna shoot me?" Ruffin asked. "Cause I ain't been shot at all day and it's getting kind of boring."

"Trust me," Morales said, "I'm trying to help you."

"I don't trust you, but I'll take that drink if you're buying."

By the time Ruffin climbed back in the car, McGrath had parked it in the lot and eaten Ruffin's bacon cheeseburger and most of his fries. Ruffin didn't mind because he counted on getting a dinner out of Morales along with his drink. "Listen," he told McGrath, "drive me down to Santa Monica and drop me off."

"You meeting a hooker?"

"None of your damn business who I'm meeting."

"Yeah, don't tell me nothing," McGrath said. "I'm just the ignorant hillbilly who chauffeurs you around like a goddam celebrity."

"And eats my cheeseburger and most of my fries."

"It's a jungle out there, Ruffin. Better get used to it."

The brew pub was a sports bar with flat-screen TVs about every three feet along the walls and a raucous crowd cursing at a dozen different teams. Morales sat waiting at the bar and when she saw Ruffin she stood up and motioned to him. He sidled up to her looking the other way like he didn't know who she was. "Let's sit in a booth," he said. "I can't afford to be seen talking to you."

"I was going to say the same thing," she said.

"Then we got that much in common already."

They found a booth in the back under a picture of Mike Tyson knocking out Michael Spinks. The waitress slapped some silverware rolled up in paper napkins on the table and started to walk away. Ruffin called after her and tried to order a couple of beers. All they had was craft beer and he'd never heard of any of them. "Two IPAs," Morales said, and the waitress went to get them.

"You see what happens to a guy in seventeen years?" Ruffin said. "I can't even order a beer."

"Parole is a period of adjustment," Morales smiled. "How's it going so far?"

Ruffin scowled. "Getting shot, insulted by the cops, chased all over town like a dog. Sort of makes Quentin feel like home."

"I'm sorry to hear that."

The waitress came back with their beers and Morales raised her glass as if in a toast. "I want you to know I'm on your side," she said, waiting for him to lift his glass. He looked in her eyes and tried to guess what she was up to. Did she really think he'd drink like that with a cop? She had pretty black eyes with something in them that was startling and unfamiliar. It had been a long time since he'd talked to somebody who wasn't afraid of him.

"I'm too thirsty to wait," she smiled again, taking a long sip.

Ruffin drained about half his glass without taking his eyes off her. "Some people want me to stay out of jail," he said. "Some want my ass back inside. Others just want to see me dead."

"That must be hard to deal with."

She sounded like the psychiatrist they sent him to before his sentencing hearing, who'd agreed and sympathized with everything he said before advising the judge to lock him up and throw away the key. Is that what was going on? What did this cop want from him? "I saw you and your partner in action," he told her. "The good cop, bad cop routine. Is that your game?"

"I don't have a game," she said.

"Course you got a game. Everybody got a game. Except maybe that slimy partner of yours."

"Burke," she nodded.

"Yeah, Burke. He don't have to play at being the bad cop. It comes natural to that bitch."

Morales didn't disagree. "Maybe I really am a good cop," she said.

"If so, then maybe you ain't as smart as you seem. How long can a good cop keep breathing in this town?"

"In my case it's going to be a while longer."

How could he respond to that? She wasn't like any cop or any woman he'd ever known. There didn't seem to be any way to provoke her. "If that's your game," he said, "maybe you ought to find another way to make a living."

Her eyes brightened. "What do you recommend? A life of crime?"

"Yeah, crime's a great gig for a cop. You don't have to learn the ropes."

They both laughed.

"So if I'm a dirty cop," she said, playing along, "I should stay on the force, earn that pension and lots of bribes along the way, but if I'm a good cop, a straight cop, I ought to throw in the towel and turn to crime. Is that it?"

"It'd be more honest, wouldn't it?"

"Honest?"

"Sure." Ruffin grinned but he was dead serious. "In this business — what you call crime, I call business — you ain't pretending to be something you ain't. You do what you got to do and that's it. You make your own rules and live by them, and you don't hurt nobody you don't have to. Everything you do is your own choice. That's honest, ain't it?"

She seemed amused by his logic. "So it's more honest to be a criminal than a cop?"

"Ain't many criminals bad as a bad cop."

Jayden stepped off the bus in the driving rain and shuffled toward the bar where he knew Alonzo would be hanging out. It was a neighborhood where he didn't like to walk around by himself, but the usual crowd wasn't outside because of the storm so nobody bothered him. He didn't bring a jacket or umbrella because that would have made him look like a pussy. By the time he reached the bar his clothes and his head were dripping wet. The bouncer scowled like he was a dog that might start shaking water all over him. "I got to see Alonzo," he told the bouncer. The bouncer nodded and stepped aside.

Alonzo sat at the bar feeding five dollar bills to one of the exotic dancers. He didn't like being interrupted. "What you doing here?" he asked Jayden without taking his eyes of the dancer.

Lights strobed and music pounded around them like the storm outside. Jayden glanced around to make sure nobody could overhear them. "That job you need done," he said. "I want to do it. I want to waste that asshole."

"You sure of that?"

"I'm sure."

Alonzo turned toward Jayden and smirked. "You know who he is?"

"Who who is?"

"That asshole you want to shoot. You know who he is?"

"I don't give a shit who he is," Jayden said. "You want me to waste him, I'll waste him."

Morales accepted Ruffin's hostility but not his argument that cops are no better than criminals. For all her frustration she still believed — she knew — that most cops were decent, honorable people who wanted to make the world a better place, even if they picked up a few crumbs for themselves along the way. She knew why she became a cop: it was a tribute to her older brother Stephen, who was killed in Afghanistan. Stephen had never wanted to be anything else but a cop, and she felt — against her mother's violent opposition — that she had to follow the path he staked out for himself. In ten years she'd seen idealistic people get sucked into the low-grade, everyday corruption of police work: nothing dramatic or cruel, just greasing the gears of the relentless machine called the criminal justice system. It was laziness as much as anything else, and boredom, and insecurity, and the inevitable victory of defeat that wore down men like Burke and made them forget why they were there. They lived under a kind of pressure the average person couldn't bear for very long, and it took its toll. But the bad ones — and she'd known a few bad ones — were no better than the criminals. She had to agree with Ruffin about that. And there was something bigger preying on her mind. Maybe it was just an overreaction to the insults she'd received for trying to do her job the way she knew it should be done, or maybe it was more than that. Why was Hague interfering, keeping her away from McGrath and that human trafficking case he'd been involved in, pushing her to pin something on Ruffin? Was he just a lazy cop like Burke who couldn't stand to see a Mexican-American woman do a better job than he would have bothered to do? Or was there a backstory there he didn't want her to find out about?

She motioned to the waitress for the check. Ruffin tried to pick it up but she stopped his hand. "I told you this would be on me," she said. She smiled mischievously. "You can pay next time."

She watched for his reaction. There wasn't any. She paid the check plus a generous tip and they walked out to her car. "Just drop me off downtown," he said, "near the train station. I can get a bus from there."

"I can give you a ride home," she said. "You'll get soaked out there."

"I'll get home all right." Obviously he didn't want her to know where he was staying.

They drove for a while but it wasn't toward the train station. She had something she wanted to show him first. A place where he could confront his past and catch a vision of the future. He'd been in a kind of limbo for seventeen years, half alive, half dead, while life went on outside. How many of those he'd left behind had died or fallen off the earth into the prison system? How many had simply disappeared? Ruffin needed to understand: there's more than one way to be dead.

The world outside was still shuddering with thunder and lightning. Morales could tell Ruffin was nervous but didn't want to show it. She drove on the freeway and headed south in the rising mist. Finally he asked: "Where the hell are you taking me?"

"You can trust me," she said. "I just want to show you something." She knew that in his mind she was first and foremost a cop, then a woman, then a Mexican, and somewhere way down on the list a human being. He had no reason to trust her in any of those categories. But the last thing he'd do was act afraid, especially since she was a woman.

"What do you think of your parole agent?" she asked him.

"Chung's a pimp who thinks I'm one of his whores. He say he owns me."

"He said that?"

"Nobody owns me."

Morales exited from the freeway and followed a street that threaded along beside it until they came to a ramp that vaulted upwards, forming an overpass. A homeless camp of tents and cardboard huts and makeshift lean-to's filled the embankment under the overpass. Morales parked a block away and they picked their way through the rain back to the camp around shells of burnt-out cars and mounds of trash, traffic noise pounding over their heads along with the rain. Morales wrapped a hooded rain jacket around her so people couldn't see her face. It wasn't raining under the overpass but water from the ramp and the freeway poured down in odd places, soaking the mattresses and sleeping bags of the less fortunate. Men huddled around fires that smoldered in metal cans as they rolled cigarettes from butts found on the street and passed around plastic milk jugs containing something that wasn't milk. They were black, white, Indian, Hispanic, Asian — Ruffin couldn't tell what most of them were — muttering together in a strange muted babble. Scarred, scared faces, unshaven for months. Teeth blackened or missing. Clothes ragged and dirty, all too big or too small. Crazy people muttering, shouting, raving. Nobody paying attention to anybody else.

He saw only one woman, aged anywhere between forty and a hundred, who pushed an overflowing grocery cart around the camp like a careful shopper. She wore several dresses layered on top of each other, which was the only reason he could tell she was a woman. For some reason she made him think of his mother, who disappeared when he was five. He couldn't remember his mother and never thought about her. Is this where she ended up? he wondered. Some place like this?

He heard a friendly voice calling out to him: "Kenny, is that you?"

An old man missing a foot hopped toward him using a broken shovel as a cane. "It's Shakey."

The last time Ruffin saw Shakey, seventeen years before, he was wearing a $600 suit and driving a Mercedes.

"Where you been?" Shakey asked. "You ain't looking so good. You been in the joint, ain't you? That what I heard."

"Seventeen years," Ruffin nodded.

"You escape? They coming after you?"

"I'm out on parole."

"You'd've been better off escaping. Least when you escape you a free man. You on parole they still own you."

Ruffin winced.

"You could live down here," Shakey said, "they never look for you here. It's a different world they don't want to know about. Least we got our freedom. Can't put a price on that."

"It's good to see you, Shakey."

"Some of the times we had!" Shakey said, spreading his toothless grin. "Remember that battle with the peckerwoods from Torrance? We kicked their asses good, didn't we? And I remember you, Kenny, you were the best of the bunch. They don't make them like you any more."

"How about you, Shakey? What you been up to?"

"How'd I end up like this, you mean?" Shakey grinned. "Well I'll tell you. Life was good, business was good, then some of them Salvadorans move in, try to squeeze me out. We take care of them, but the cops want a bigger piece and I can't pay, I'm in over my head with crack and heroin and pills, and I still can't pay. Then one night the cops grab me and throw me in a ambulance and smash my foot with their sticks and the hospital chops it off. Ain't nothing wrong with it before that but they smash it up and chop it off, just to warn me, they say, and when I get back I'm on crutches and my gang won't look at me. Get out of our sight, they tell me, and my ho's hooked up with that Earvin — you remember him? — who set the whole thing up with the cops. They drop me off down here like I'm a dead man. I don't know how many years ago that was. I had to fight, lost all my teeth but I put a few gangbangers in the ground myself so I got respect here. They don't go after me no more and the cops don't come down here. Least I'm a free man."

A few other men circled in the shadows, listening without joining in. Shakey pointed to one of them, a scarecrow in a knit cap who stood clutching a black plastic garbage bag. "You remember Monty, don't you?" Shakey asked.

"Sure, I remember Monty." Ruffin stepped toward him — they'd been friends, grew up on the same block — but Monty lowered his eyes and slipped back into the shadows.

"Monty did a ten year stretch," Shakey said, "after his lady lawyer sold him out — turned his heroin business over to the Pagans when they put a contract out on her kids."

Shakey motioned toward a pile of rags on one of the mattresses. "Enrique over there" — Ruffin remembered Enrique — "used to be big in the Mexican gangs but he got caught in a shoot-out and lost his balls and half of his ass."

A bearded white guy with a ponytail leaned forward to warm his hands over a pile of burning trash. "That's Lionel," Shakey said. The man didn't look up. "Lionel started out as a accountant and got hosed big time by the judge who was supposed to give him a slap on the wrist."

Ruffin saw one man he'd been hoping never to see again: Tremaine Jordan. Ruffin had messed up Tremaine in a fight when they were both about nineteen and he'd sworn to kill Ruffin if he ever saw him again. His hollow eyes stayed on Ruffin until Ruffin nodded to him, then he turned away and disappeared into the jungle of tents without a look back. Ruffin wasn't afraid of Tremaine but he had a bad feeling, a twinge of regret for what he'd done to him. Was that what brought Tremaine to this place? If the fight had gone the other way — if Ruffin hadn't done what he did to Tremaine — would he be here instead?

"Who's your ho?" Shakey asked, squinting at Morales. "She look like a cop in that jacket."

"She ain't no cop," Ruffin said. "Just a ho I picked up."

Morales pulled her hood closer around her face.

"Better get her out of here," Shakey said in a low voice. "We don't get too many women down here and they don't last long."

The drive back was silent for the first ten minutes. They listened to the trucks roaring past and the rain beating down and the tires splashing over the freeway and they watched the lights in the rain and the mist. The thunder and lightning had moved south over the ocean. It was like waking up after a nightmare.

"Okay," Ruffin finally said. "You gonna tell me what you want from me?"

"I thought that was obvious," Morales said. "I was hoping you could help me find whoever shot you and that little girl and her mother. Before they kill somebody else."

"Can't you solve your own case without me?"

"I guess I forget to tell you." She kept her eyes on the road straight ahead. "I'm off the case. Maybe out of a job."

More silence, but of a different kind: puzzlement, embarrassment, expectation.

"They took you off the case?"

"Yeah, and you know why?" Morales said. "Because I didn't want to use you as a decoy and maybe let you get killed."

She turned off the freeway at East Commercial and turned at Alameda toward the train station.

"Well, I found the guy that did the shooting," Ruffin said, "so you can stop following me around."

She glanced in his direction. "You know who it was?"

"Yeah, but I ain't gonna tell you."

"You'd rather kill him than snitch on him?"

"I ain't gonna snitch. But I ain't gonna kill him neither."

She pulled up along the curb near Union Station to let him out. She left the engine running and the wipers swishing but disconnected her seat belt so she could turn around to face him. "Why aren't you going to kill him?"

"You met Shanise. She the mother of my son."

"Nice lady."

"I been in San Quentin seventeen years and I ain't met nobody like Shanise." Ruffin looked a little sheepish when he mentioned Shanise. "She give me a good talking to."

18

Ruffin woke up the next morning to sunlight streaming through the window of his little bedroom and the din of country music jangling in through the window. McGrath had the Cadillac backed up to the rundown garage behind the sister's house with the radio on and the trunk lid open. Singing some redneck song along with the music, he lifted a case of Snapple iced tea out of the trunk and opened all twenty-four bottles. He poured them out, one by one, and watched the iced tea run down the driveway. The tar on the driveway was broken into chunks, with weeds and cactus and anthills between the chunks, and there was plenty of room for the iced tea to sink in. It was a hot, steamy morning after all the rain the night before.

"I could use a drink of that iced tea," Ruffin said, stepping out the back door. "Why you pouring it out?"

"Keep your panties on," McGrath said. He reached into the trunk and lifted out a five-gallon gas can. He filled the 24 iced-tea bottles with gasoline, screwed on their caps and arranged them back in the cardboard case. They looked like they'd never been opened.

"What's this?" Ruffin asked.

"You never seen a Molotov cocktail?"

"You starting a war?"

"This is the day I'm gonna get my money," McGrath said. He tossed a box of kitchen matches into the trunk. "If there's any trouble we'll be ready for it."

Ruffin took a step back in case the bombs exploded.

"Cops search the car," McGrath went on, "they won't find no weapons." He set the gas-filled bottles gently down in the trunk. "Just a case of Snapple iced tea."

He opened a new bottle of Wild Turkey and took a swig. "How's that shoulder doing?" He reached for the duct tape. "You need another treatment?"

"It's okay," Ruffin said, wincing at the memory of his last treatment.

Venturing into the dingy garage, McGrath came out with an armful of gardening tools that looked like torture implements. A long-handled hedge clipper. A knifelike spade. A hand cultivator with claw-like tines. "In case you were wondering, these ain't weapons neither," he said.

"They're for gardening," Ruffin said.

"Right, gardening," McGrath agreed. "That's a wholesome, healthful occupation for a couple of ex-cons, ain't it?" He dropped the tools in the trunk and Ruffin followed him into the shadowy garage.

"You think we gonna need all this shit?" Ruffin asked.

"You never can tell," McGrath said. "The young kids today are nasty, nastier than we ever were. Hand me them wire cutters, would you?"

Ruffin handed him a pair of wire cutters that hung on the wall. McGrath tried fitting the blades around his fingers — they would have fit just right to snip them off — and tossed them in the trunk.

"Can you blame them kids?" Ruffin said. "They look at the justice system and what they see ain't nothing like justice. They look at cops and politicians and see criminals that never go to jail. They go out on parole and find out they gotta do crime or do time."

McGrath picked up a length of rope and coiled it up before dropping it in the trunk. "You're preaching to the choir, brother," he said. "I been saying that for years. Kids today got no sense of right and wrong. You and me, we got that beat into us before we was five years old."

He found a heavy wooden axe handle, tried a couple of vicious swings, and clunked it into the trunk. "I always tell young people, being a criminal ain't a walk in the park. If you're gonna live outside the law, you gotta know the difference between right and wrong. If not, you're gonna make some big mistakes."

His next find was a pair of fishing rods, a big plastic tackle box full of lures and hooks and spools of line, and a canvas fishing vest with a dozen pockets and pouches. "Fishing," he said. "That's another peaceful hobby for the law abiding citizen."

The fishing gear clattered into the trunk. "I had a young punk working for me once, wanted to waste a nun," McGrath said. "You hear that? Waste a nun, right in her nun's habit in front of the church. I said no, we can't do that. He says, why not? We're criminals, ain't we? We can do whatever we want."

"You believe that?" Ruffin asked.

"Hell, no. A criminal's got to set limits for himself, since nobody else is doing it for him. You can't just fall back on what's legal and what's not. You got to decide for yourself what's the right thing to do."

"That's true," Ruffin agreed.

"You Catholic?" McGrath asked.

"No, I ain't."

"Me neither. But hell, even without being Catholic I knew that wasting a nun was a bad idea."

He slammed the trunk lid shut and they climbed into the Cadillac. McGrath took a swig of Wild Turkey and gunned the engine. "And you know what?" he said. "It turned out I was right. That nun was working undercover, packing a Magnum .44."

They stopped at Denny's for breakfast and McGrath had a lot more to say about the state of the world and all the things he'd do after he collected his money. Ruffin grunted a lot of Uh-huh's but his mind was back in that homeless camp with Shakey and Monty and Enrique, wondering if this nightmare world was where he'd end up. He believed in fate and so far his fate had always been a hard one. If he was granted another chance at life, what would it even look like?

"Today's your lucky day, Ruffin," McGrath said. "The day I collect my money."

"Why's that lucky for me?"

"You stick with me and you'll find out."

McGrath couldn't stop talking about the Molotov cocktails and how he planned to use them if he didn't get his money. The last thing Ruffin wanted was to be lured into his crazy schemes. But there was no danger of that. It wasn't like McGrath was some kind of mastermind who could charm him into doing something he didn't want to do. Low cunning was as high as McGrath could jump.

"Why won't somebody come after you if they know you got all that money?" Ruffin asked.

"Where I'm going," McGrath said, "Sherlock Holmes couldn't find me."

"I guess you're pretty smart."

"Just smart enough to know my limitations. I ain't the Napoleon of crime, or even the Julius Caesar."

"Maybe the Donald Trump," Ruffin suggested.

"That's about right. My mama used to say if I had a brain I'd be dangerous."

A solitary thought ruled McGrath's dangerous brain. He wanted his money and he wanted it now. He knew that pressing the issue could be — was sure to be — hazardous to his health. But he had a plan, a grand plan he meant to consummate that very afternoon, in which his new friend Kenny Ruffin, without knowing it, would play a crucial part. He just needed Ruffin to stick with him one more day. No need to compensate him for services he didn't even know he was rendering. But there was someone else McGrath would need help from, and her he'd have to pay.

They cruised past the same gas stations and cheap motels and strip malls as the day before. McGrath cut a sharp left into the parking lot by the Chinese restaurant where they'd met Chung.

"We going to see Chung again?" Ruffin asked.

"Nah," McGrath said, "I just need to talk to my girlfriend a minute."

They saw Kimberly in the alley walking toward the back parking lot. McGrath jumped out and ran to catch up with her. "I'm late for a meeting," she told him.

"A meeting?" he said. "What are you, a goddam alcoholic?"

She winked. "It's with a guy named John."

"Darlin,'" he said, "if you help me with something, I'll give you a lot more than you can make peddling your pretty little ass."

"It's sweet of you to call my ass little and pretty," she said, "when you know damn well it's fat and ugly. But you won't be getting another piece of it till you tell me what happened to that Chinese girl."

"I told you, that's private information."

"I bet you don't even know who strangled her."

"Sure I know. Why do you think they promised me all that money for lying about it? You help me out, I'll give you a share of it."

"What kind of share?"

"Five thousand if everything goes without a hitch."

She motioned for him to follow her around the corner. They stood next to the dumpster where nobody could see them. "What do you want me to do?"

"Tell Chung to get the money from his uncle," McGrath said. "Then you bring it to me. I'll tell you where later."

"I don't have enough gas in my van to drive anywhere."

He reached in his pocket and handed her a twenty dollar bill. "It'll be downtown where there's lots of people around, so nobody's tempted to try anything stupid. Come alone."

"You coming alone?" she asked.

"I'm bringing Ruffin, and he'll be armed and dangerous like he always is. I ain't gonna be a sitting duck."

"Ruffin'll defend both of us if something goes wrong?"

"Damn right he will. I told you he's like a wild animal. Enjoys fighting and killing for its own sake."

"Okay," she said. "I'll talk to Chung."

"Tell him it's a hundred grand now. That's what they owe me with eight years interest added on."

She walked toward her van and McGrath called after her. "And tell him if I don't get that money today, the whole story's going on the TV news tomorrow."

While McGrath was talking to McGrath, Ruffin's phone buzzed and Morales said hello. "What you want now?" Ruffin said.

"Can you meet me in Hancock Park in an hour?" Morales asked.

"Hancock Park? You mean the tar pits?"

He remembered Hancock Park from a school trip when he was a kid. It had a museum and some sludge ponds they called the La Brea Tar Pits where some dinosaurs got stuck before they went extinct. At least that was how he remembered it. He also recalled a statue of two sabretooth tigers fighting to the death, which was fresh in his mind because in San Quentin there was a lifer the guards called Sabretooth on account of his metal front teeth.

"Why you always inviting me to some graveyard?" he asked Morales. "First that homeless camp, and now the tar pits. You think I'm some kind of dinosaur?"

"At least at this one," she laughed, "you won't see anybody you know."

In her van after McGrath had left, Kimberly sat with her phone to her ear. "I'm supposed to meet him downtown with a hundred grand, some place where there's a lot of people around," she said into the phone. "Ruffin's gonna be there too. Armed and dangerous, McGrath says."

She listened for a while and said: "I don't know where exactly. He's gonna call me later. You want me to talk to Chung? Okay, I'll call him and he can talk to his uncle."

19

Ruffin and Morales sat on a bench near the La Brea Tar Pits Museum in Hancock Park. It's a leafy park on Wilshire Boulevard with paved paths and a modernistic museum that sits next to a sludge pond. Morales had brought some take-out food in a white paper bag which she shared with Ruffin. She nibbled a cheeseburger while Ruffin ate a chicken sandwich. Outside their set roles as cop and criminal they enjoyed each other's company. They shared pleasantries and jokes before the conversation turned serious.

"I was hoping you'd reconsider helping me identify the shooter," Morales said.

"I ain't snitching," Ruffin said.

"There are ways you could do it without being a snitch."

"I ain't snitching, one way or the other. That man been warned. He been more than warned."

"Is it somebody you know?" she asked.

"Just some kid wants to be big dawg in the neighborhood."

"Who's he working for?"

"I don't know if he's working for anybody. He's got his own crew, guns, a nice car. Maybe he's working for himself."

Ruffin didn't believe that. Alonzo was just some kid who was going to Lucille's pre-school when Ruffin went inside. Maybe he wanted to be big dawg in the neighborhood but he wasn't there yet, just a gangbanger wannabe with a posse of teenage punks who ought to be in school. Ruffin wouldn't snitch and he wasn't going to kill him, but his motives weren't all humanitarian. He wanted to find out who Alonzo was working for. There had to be somebody behind him, somebody a lot bigger who'd still be there if he got wasted. But Ruffin wasn't going to mention that to Morales. Let her think he was acting on principle before moving on to other things.

She motioned for him to keep quiet as a woman with a baby stroller sat down on the next bench. She and Ruffin stood up and walked toward the museum, stopping in front of the statue of the sabretooth tigers. "Are you sure there isn't more to it than that?" Morales asked.

"What're you thinking?"

"There's something that's not right about this," she said. "The police jumped right on you about the shooting, like it was your fault."

"That's what I been saying."

"Why are they so against you?"

Why were the cops against him? He pointed to the statue. "Why're those two sabretooth tigers at each other's throats?"

She looked back at him and shrugged. It was one of those questions that didn't have an answer.

"I got a history," Ruffin said. "Remember? I just got out of San Quentin."

"Parole," Morales said.

"That's what they call it. And before that—well, let's just say I got a history."

Next to the museum was the tar pit, a big gurgling pool of sludge with fake life-size mastodons set up along the edge and out in the middle as if they were sinking into the tar. Giant bubbles that looked like human heads rose to the top, burst and disappeared. They reminded Ruffin of a movie he'd seen about real-looking people who grew out of pods like plants. They weren't real people, of course, but soulless shells that looked and acted just like everybody else.

"What about McGrath?" Morales asked. "What's he been doing since he got out?"

"The fool's been trying to collect some money Chung's uncle owes him from before he went inside."

Morales laughed. "Chung's uncle owes him money?"

"A lot of money. Chung knew all about it too."

"Did McGrath say why?"

"No," Ruffin said, "and I never asked." He never asked and now he got a sinking feeling when he thought about it. He knew more than he could tell Morales about Chung's uncle and the people he did business with. They weren't the type who'd let a babbling fool like McGrath walk around with any of their secrets in his pocket.

Ruffin and Morales stood at the edge of the tar pit looking through the fence at the sludge and the fake mastodons and the bursting bubbles that looked like people trying to hatch. The place smelled like an oil refinery. "There's something dirty going on in the department," Morales said, "and I'm going to find out what it is."

"Something dirtier than usual?"

"I thought maybe you could help me clean it up."

It was Ruffin's turn to laugh. "Help you clean up the police department? Ain't enough hours in my day to do that."

They moved away from the pond, away from the museum, toward a grove of palm trees at the other end of the park.

"Don't get me wrong," Ruffin said. "I hate cops — nothing personal — but even the bad ones, they ain't no different from anybody else. They greedy, they violent, they evil, that's just the way folks are."

"Most cops are good people," Morales said.

"Then — not counting you — I guess I only know the bad ones."

"The bad ones are worse than criminals. You said so yourself."

"They're worse," Ruffin said, "but they still ain't no different from anybody else."

She stopped walking and looked into his eyes. She knew there was a good man in there if she could only connect with him. "Kenny — do you mind if I call you Kenny? — I'm asking you to help me with this."

Ruffin didn't like being stared at that way and he didn't want her calling him Kenny. "With what?"

"Whatever's going on in the department." She touched his sleeve. "It's got something to do with you and they're keeping me away from it."

"It ain't got nothing to do with me," he said. But to himself he wondered if she could be right. What Chung had warned him about — no, that was impossible. It was all too long ago.

"I want to find out what it is," Morales said.

"You don't know me," he told her. "I don't help cops."

"I don't help ex-cons. But I've gone out of my way to help you."

"So far all you done is take me to a homeless camp and a smelly tar pit where I could go by myself if I wanted to. Which I don't."

"I'm probably going to lose my job because I tried to keep them from using you as a decoy."

Ruffin turned away and continued toward a clump of palm trees until she came up beside him. "Maybe that's helping me, maybe not," he said.

"What do you mean?"

"If I ain't a decoy, don't that make me one of the ducks?"

Morales offered Ruffin a ride and when he squeezed himself into her car she could tell he was in pain. "The shoulder bothering you?" she asked.

"A little."

"When was the last time you had it looked at?"

"Yesterday morning," Ruffin said. "McGrath poured some Wild Turkey on it and wrapped it up in duct tape."

When he refused to go back to the hospital, she drove a few blocks to her apartment. "Come on in and I'll change that dressing."

"I ain't going in your apartment."

"Don't worry," she told him. "None of your friends are going to see you here."

Morales was hoping none of her friends would see them either. She'd never done anything like this before — bringing a felon who'd just been released from prison to her apartment. Was she crazy? But there was no reason she couldn't do this.

She'd been taken off the shooting case and Ruffin wasn't a suspect in anything, just an ordinary citizen, a crime victim actually, who needed help. She'd had advanced first aid training as part of her police work and it was perfectly appropriate to help him with the bandage. She liked him, she didn't know why. Physically, yes, but it was more than that. She liked his spirit, his determination not to be a broken man. He was walking on the edge, trying to keep from slipping. They were a lot alike (crazy as it sounded for her to think that), both trying to hang onto their self-respect as they fought back, without fighting back any more than they needed to, because that would make them look weak and put them at risk. Maybe helping him out was her way of sticking it to the department, telling them they didn't own her, they couldn't dictate how she lived her life.

Her apartment was a one-bedroom on the tenth floor of a modern building. Ruffin sat down on a kitchen chair and took off his shirt. She had to hack at the duct tape with scissors for five minutes to get it off, and it left toxic-looking glue all over his shoulder. The gauze under the tape was bloody and black, and the wound was oozing blood and pus. She wiped off the blood and doused the wound with hydrogen peroxide.

"What's that shit?" Ruffin asked.

"Hydrogen peroxide," she said. "It's a lot cheaper than Wild Turkey but it does the same thing. Don't drink it, though."

Bubbles fizzed up in a white foam, indicating an infection. She irrigated the wound until the fizzing stopped, then she wrapped it in gauze and taped it over with sterile tape, scraping off as much of the glue as she could. "You should have this done every day," she said. "Preferably at the hospital. And don't use duct tape."

"I ain't going back there."

"You could come here then." She laid her hand on his other shoulder and left it there a little too long.

He stood up and pulled his shirt back on. "Don't you worry about me. I'll be just fine."

20

The Commissioner sat reading on his couch beside an attractive, much younger woman clad only in bra and panties. She was an administrative assistant on the third floor who wanted to advance in her career. To do so she had to submit to what the Commissioner called "mentoring" (a common form of mandatory on-the-job training in L.A.). She planted a kiss on his blotchy face, but with his book in one hand (he was on page 698 of *Being and Nothingness*) and his phone in the other he hardly seemed to notice. The phone played a ring tone that sounded like Sinatra singing "My Way." The screen said it was Hague.

"Today's another day, Hague," the Commissioner said into the phone. "What have you got for me?"

"I've got some good news, sir," Hague said. "The little girl is out of danger."

"What little girl is that?"

"The one who was shot getting off the bus with Ruffin and McGrath."

The Commissioner tossed his book down, pushed the woman aside and flew into a rage. "What planet are you on, Hague?" he shouted. "I don't give a shit about that little girl."

An elderly Chinese businessman — it was Harold Chung's uncle — hunched over his desk in a cramped Chinatown office, arguing with his nephew on the phone. Since he had no son, he'd had to settle for this fat, asthmatic, effeminate nephew, a disgrace to the family from his earliest days who'd compounded his disgrace by joining the Department of Corrections as a parole agent. In that guise, he boasted to the uncle, he could dabble in the rackets without taking any risk, having an obedient army of convicted felons at his command. And when the need arose he could facilitate communications with the cops and the criminal bosses and the politicians, disreputable elements of society which the uncle's business required him to deal with. Now his nephew was trying to help him extricate himself from a situation he'd been sucked into about eight years before in one of his hotels. A girl was strangled and the gangsters who ran the human trafficking racket had promised an unstable petty crook named McGrath fifty thousand dollars for lying about it, and after eight years in the slammer he wanted double that amount or he'd spill his guts to the media. This would not be good, not for the gangsters who'd promised McGrath the fifty thousand (the uncle and his nephew were careful never to mention any names), not for the cops who protected the underage prostitution racket over the years, not for the strangler whose depravity had triggered the whole fiasco, and least of all for the old man, who wanted to spend his declining years in peace. But how much of this could you discuss on the phone? All of it, if you made it sound like you were talking about the Hao Yun restaurant and the demands of its eccentric chef. Even an FBI cryptographer fluent in Chinese couldn't have deciphered the conversation the old man had on the phone with his nephew that afternoon.

"I talked to the noodle supplier about the chef's demand for more noodles," the uncle said in Chinese. "He wasn't too happy about that."

"We're going to need those noodles," Chung said. "You know what the chef is like. So temperamental — crazy, actually — and unpredictable. He says he needs a hundred pounds of noodles or he'll go on "Good Morning America" and talk about that waitress who choked on the Russian dressing."

"The noodle supplier says he can't spare that many noodles," the uncle complained. "Only the fifty pounds in the original order. And only if I agree to supply another fifty pounds of noodles from one of my other restaurants."

"They won't deliver their fifty pounds unless you supply fifty?"

"That's right," the uncle said. "It's like they think we're partners, even though they're the ones who recommended that waitress and supplied the Russian dressing. All I did was give the girl a place to work. Does that make me their partner?"

"Do you have fifty pounds of noodles lying around?" Chung asked.

"I do," the uncle said, "and I'm willing to put them in the stir-fry if that will keep the restaurant running smoothly. But there's one other condition. They want you to pick up their fifty pounds and my fifty pounds and personally deliver the whole order to the chef, wherever he wants to meet you. To make sure he really gets the noodles and won't go on TV to talk about that waitress."

Kimberly sashayed through the front door of the Chinese restaurant like she owned the place and spotted Chung hulking behind his usual table in the corner. A couple hours earlier she'd relayed McGrath's ultimatum over the phone. Chung told her he needed to talk to his uncle, and now she'd come to hear the answer. Chung was furious when she planted the tail end of her mini-skirt on the chair across from him. "You can't come in here dressed like that," he said.

"Entry in rear for the whores?"

"No entry at all as far as I'm concerned."

"I believe it," she smirked. She crossed her legs and the mini-skirt rode even farther upward. "Did you talk to your uncle?"

Chung kept one eye on Felipe behind the bar, who watched impassively, awaiting his command. "My uncle's willing to do this if it'll get rid of McGrath once and for all," Chung said.

"I can just about guarantee that," Kimberly laughed.

"What do you mean?"

"He told me as soon as he gets the money he's going a long ways away. Belize or someplace."

"Thank God for that," Chung said.

She opened her tiny purse, extracted a cigarette, and started to light it.

"What the hell are you doing?" Chung asked.

"You didn't know whores smoked?" she laughed. "You need to get out more."

"There's no smoking in here."

"You sure are puritanical for a pimp," she said.

"I'm not a pimp." Chung's eyes flashed. "I'm a public servant helping desperate women land on their feet."

"On their feet isn't exactly where we're landing," Kimberly laughed. "But I guess it's all right as long as we don't smoke in your restaurant."

"It's the law. You ought to know that."

She laughed again. "That's a good one."

"Lower your voice, will you?"

She puffed some smoke in his direction. Felipe started toward her but Chung waved him off. "Please," he said. "I have COPD." He pointed to the oxygen tanks next to the table.

"Your uncle can come up with a hundred thousand dollars on a couple of hours' notice?" Kimberly said.

"My uncle is a very thrifty man," Chung said, coughing. "He can afford to go along with this plan." It was part of the subterfuge that all the money was coming from the uncle. "But here's the thing: I have to be the one who makes the drop."

"You don't trust me?"

"You can come along," Chung said, "but I'll be carrying the money. And Felipe will be watching my back."

"Okay," she said. "I mean I think it's okay. Why not? McGrath said come alone, but why should he care as long as he gets his money? I don't know about Felipe, though. Things could get ugly with him in the picture. No offense, Felipe."

"Felipe goes where I go," Chung insisted. He coughed again.

"I don't know," Kimberly said, crushing her cigarette in a tea cup.

"If McGrath doesn't like that, I'll send Felipe by himself," Chung said. "Only in that case he won't be bringing any money."

McGrath held the steering wheel with his elbows as he dialed his phone with both hands. It seemed awkward, even dangerous, but how else were you supposed to do it? At least he didn't have any trouble remembering Kimberly's number. It was the only one he knew.

"Yeah?" she grunted. It wasn't the friendly, inviting way you'd expect a hooker to answer the phone. Good thing she didn't have a 900 number. He could hear traffic noise in the background. She must have been in her van.

"Okay, here's the drill," he said. "Meet me with the money at Bank of America Plaza. Six o'clock, under the golden arches."

"What is it? A McDonalds?"

"It's got golden arches, don't it? What do you think it is, the Burger King? Be there at six on the dot. A hundred thousand in a satchel. Is the uncle on board?"

"Yeah, he's got the money, believe it or not," Kimberly said. "But Chung wants to come along, with his bodyguard. Felipe."

"No dice."

"He says that's the only way he'll do it. If you don't like it, he says he'll send Felipe by himself. Without any money."

"What's that supposed to mean?"

"You ever see this Felipe? It means you better go through with your plan or Felipe's gonna make you wish you didn't get out of bed this morning."

"The deal's off."

"Listen, Chung's got the money. Isn't that what you want?"

A moment of silence while McGrath thought it over.

"Okay," he said. "You can bring Chung and his girlfriend. But there better not be any other horseshit or the deal's off. You can tell him that. This is gonna be in a public place with lots of people watching. And Ruffin's gonna be there as *my* bodyguard."

Only Ruffin don't know that yet, McGrath chuckled to himself.

"That man don't take any shit," he added. "He'll chop Felipe up into a pile of chicken liver at the first sign of trouble. Does Chung understand that?"

"Yeah, I think so," Kimberly said. "Now, when do I get my cut?"

"You walk up and hand me the bag and we'll go back to my car to divvy it up," McGrath said.

"You think you're gonna take me back to your car?"

"How else are we gonna do it?"

"Like I'm a hostage or something?"

"What the hell are you talking about?"

"Listen, asswipe," Kimberly said. "My cut just went up to ten thousand. You better give it to me on the spot with no bullshit or I'll be all over you like flies on a turd."

"Yeah," McGrath growled before he slammed his cell phone down on the steering wheel. "Which one are you? The flies or the turd?"

21

Julie Morales had a friend named Brian Epstein who was an Assistant District Attorney. They'd dated a few times but the relationship didn't go anywhere. A cop and a lawyer never see eye to eye, it turned out, even about where to have dinner. Still they'd remained friends. She called him and asked if she could see him at his office on a work-related matter. That was partly true, she told herself. Her interest in McGrath was work-related, even if she'd been taken off the case. It was the reason she might lose her job.

Brian had been on the prosecution team for the human trafficking and prostitution cases arising from the death of the Chinese girl in Chung's uncle's hotel. "Do I remember Cat McGrath?" he laughed when Morales had settled into a chair across from his desk and explained why she was there. "For a few months, eight years ago, I was spending half my time with that slime bucket."

"That must have been fun."

"I heard he was getting out of prison. Is he causing trouble already?"

"It's not clear," Morales said. "He's peripheral to something I'm working on. I'm trying to find out how he fit into that human trafficking case. Do you still have a transcript of his testimony?"

"You can read the transcript if you want to," Brian said, "but I'll spare you the agony. I was there for the whole trial. Sometimes I was the one asking the questions, and let me tell you, the pile of horseshit he dumped in that courtroom was so deep, we had to take turns questioning him or we would have choked on the stench."

"It was Judge Garver, wasn't it?"

"Yes," Brian said, "and I've never seen her so bent out of shape. McGrath was on the stand for three days. He wouldn't stop talking but he said next to nothing. Every question you asked, you got the story of his life. Pure bullshit. Dodged every direct question and finessed every indirect one. For three whole days he stuck to his self-contradictions and dug himself deeper into a hole with every sentence."

"Just plain lying?"

"No question about it. The judge yelled at him, held him in contempt, put him in jail, but he never wavered. Then she revoked his parole and sent him back to San Quentin for ten years."

"So what's the explanation?" Morales asked.

"Witness tampering, obviously. He had no personal interest in lying. He'd been granted immunity."

"Somebody threatened him?"

"Or paid him off. Both, most likely."

"Who do you think he was protecting?" Morales asked.

"That's the mystery. Certainly not the old man — the old Chinese man who owned the hotel. He was on trial for his involvement in the human trafficking and prostitution but he wasn't a suspect in the actual murder. We had no suspect for that."

"But you put the old man on trial anyway?"

"Yeah." Brian lowered his voice. "There was some kind of power struggle going on between the D.A's office and the police."

"Nothing unusual about that," Morales said.

"Except this was at the highest level. The scuttlebutt was that the D.A. thought the police were protecting somebody, and the Police Commissioner threatened to go public with some dirt on the D.A. if he said that in public. We gave McGrath an immunity deal in hopes that he would talk."

Morales laughed. "Be careful what you wish for."

Brian had to laugh too. "He talked, all right, but he didn't give us any smoking guns. He admitted that he took the girl to the room where her body was found. Claimed he thought he was taking her there to be interviewed for secretarial school. And he swore that the man who greeted them at the door was a Russian."

"How did he know the guy was Russian?"

"Good question. We spent about half a day on that. He couldn't name a single actual Russian he'd ever met or talked to, or say a single Russian word, not even *da* or *nyet*. He once spent a night in jail in Moscow, Idaho, and he knew how much vodka to put in a Black Russian. That was about all he knew about Russians."

"So the Russian was never found," Morales said.

"There was no Russian staying at the hotel or anywhere near it. The police talked to every Russian tourist in the area that fit McGrath's description, although — that's another thing: his descriptions were all over the map. Age? First it was forty, then fifty, then sixty. Hair color? Blond, black, gray. You get the idea. His testimony was a three-day exercise in alternative reality."

"Lying, in other words."

"Which, by the way, McGrath does very well. He's one of those people who can look you in the eye and tell a barefaced lie and almost make you believe it, even when you know it couldn't possibly be true."

"One of those people?" Morales asked.

"Yeah," Brian said. "They're called sociopaths."

When McGrath parked in front of Grijalva's sister's house, he thought there was something different about it. Same peeling paint, same crumbling cement in the steps, same garbage and knee-high weeds in the yard. The windows were shut, the blinds down just as he'd left them. Still there was something suspicious about the place. He looked up and down the street for strange cars — all the ones he saw were old, battered, souped up, just like before. No unmarked cop cars or hitmen's SUVs. Cautiously, he stepped up to the front door and stuck his key in the lock.

The door flew open and there she was in the flesh, Grijalva's sister. Even hotter than in her picture, in short shorts and a halter top, but without the come hither smile. In fact she wasn't smiling at all. She was shoving a twelve-gauge pump action Remington into his face.

"You must be Grijalva's sister," he said.

"You must be the latest scumbag my piece of shit brother sent to whack me." She herded him through the door and followed him inside. "Down on your knees," she said.

McGrath did as he was told, hands over his head. He peeked upwards as he pled for his life. "You got this all wrong," he said.

"You're the tenth one he sent here," the sister said. "Numbers one through nine are buried in the basement."

"I came here to warn you. I heard your brother recruiting killers in San Quentin and I wanted to warn you."

"Don't bullshit me."

She leveled the shotgun two inches from his forehead.

"Sweetheart," McGrath said in his twangiest voice, "in about two hours I'm coming into a shitload of money, more money than you ever imagined in your wildest dreams. If you don't shoot me I'll split it with you. Fifty fifty."

"Eighty twenty," she said. She cocked the shotgun and adjusted her aim.

"I got a better idea," he said. "Soon as I get my money I'm running off to Belize. How'd you like to come along?"

Derek began his day early, sailing out the door at dawn before Shanise woke up. He drove his red F-150 pickup to the FedEx distribution center near LAX and ran deliveries for nine hours, returning home by 4:00. That morning, before he left the house, he'd checked Jayden's room and found the bed unslept in. He called Shanise during his lunch hour.

"I saw him before I left for work," she said. "He must have come home after you left."

"He's coming home at six in the morning? What the hell is he doing all night?"

"I don't know," Shanise said. She might have sounded indifferent but she wasn't. She just hated being a buffer strip in the war between Derek and Jayden. "Why don't you ask him?"

Derek had a better idea. He decided to wait for Jayden to come home and then follow him the next time he went out. If he had to physically restrain him, beat him silly, drag him through the streets until he came to his senses, that's what he would do. It was for the boy's own good. Derek would do just about anything to keep Jayden's life from being swallowed up by criminals or (what was probably worse) the so-called criminal justice system. In his younger days — before he joined the Marines — he'd had some experience of his own with that system that Shanise didn't even know about.

He waited in the garage behind the house, where he kept his pride and joy: his red F-150 pickup. And his guns.

Alonzo Payne cruised the back streets of South Los Angeles in his black BMW as he got his mental shit together for what would go down that afternoon. After what Ruffin did to him at Wellington's his only thought was to wipe that man off the earth. There was no torture too painful for that prick. He was dangerous, anxious to prove he could survive on the street — that's why one of them pussies hanging around on the front porch needed to take him out. If somebody got to die, let it be one of them. Then the man called, the one who told him to shoot at the bus in the first place. He said back off, they got a different plan now. That's yesterday, today they change their mind again. The man calls back and says six o'clock, Bank of America Plaza. Be there. Wait for instructions. What they need me there for? To shoot somebody or be shot? To wait for instructions while they do their killing so they got somebody to pin it on?

Jayden better come along. He don't even know who that man is he's supposed to shoot, and he don't want to know. I ain't gonna be the one to tell him. If they shoot him he don't ever need to find out.

22

Morales had dropped Ruffin back at Hancock Park before she went to Brian Epstein's office. As soon as she finished with Brian she dialed Ruffin's cell phone number. "Where are you?" she asked.

"Still sitting in the park," Ruffin said. He'd bought an ice cream and he sat on a bench along Wilshire waiting for McGrath to pick him up.

"Where's McGrath?" Morales asked.

"On his way over to pick me up."

"I think I found out where that money he wants is coming from," Morales said.

"Chung's uncle," Ruffin said. "I told you that."

"Yes, but why does Chung's uncle owe it to him?"

"I told you, he didn't say."

"Do you know how much money it is?"

"He didn't say that neither."

"Okay," Morales said. "Here's what I found out. About eight years ago there was a local tragedy that attracted a lot of attention in the media. A Chinese girl about fourteen years old was found dead in one of Chung's uncle's hotels. She'd come off a ship docked in Long Beach bringing young girls to the U.S. for sexual exploitation. Human trafficking but the girls didn't know it until they got here."

"I heard about that set-up long ago," Ruffin said. "Before I went inside."

"Really? It went on for that long?"

"You cops are always so surprised at the things that go on out here," Ruffin said. "Even when you get paid for letting them happen."

There was an uncomfortable silence before Morales continued. "How much do you know about this?" she asked.

"Just what I heard on the street," Ruffin said. He didn't want to go into what he knew about it, or how. "And most of that I already forgot. But what are you saying? You saying McGrath killed this girl?"

"No, I'm not saying that," Morales said. "But some pervert got hold of her and strangled her — intentionally or not, nobody knows — in that hotel room. Chung's uncle was arrested on prostitution and human trafficking charges and went to trial. McGrath was identified by a desk clerk as the one who brought the girl to the hotel."

"That why he went up to Quentin?" Ruffin asked.

"Yeah," Morales said. "He claimed he was just the driver and didn't know anything about the prostitution. But he did know something about who the murderer was. He said the man he brought the girl to was a Russian. The police couldn't find any trace of a Russian, but McGrath stuck with his story even after they gave him immunity. He was on the witness stand for three days."

"In three days he'd just be getting around to giving his name and address."

"That's about right," Morales said. "I didn't read the transcript but I'm told by an Assistant D.A. that it was obvious to everybody in the courtroom that McGrath was lying through his teeth."

"McGrath's been lying through his teeth since before he had teeth."

"He was protecting somebody — the D.A.'s office got into a behind-the-scenes battle with the department about that — and he was probably supposed to get paid for it. But the judge sent him to prison before he could get paid. Whoever he was protecting is the one that owes him the money."

"Chung's uncle?"

"Sounds like it, doesn't it?"

Ruffin wasn't a bit surprised. "I'll tell you this much," he said. "McGrath plans on getting that money today."

"Are you sure?"

"This afternoon. About two hours from now."

"Are you helping him with that?"

"He thinks I am. He keeps telling me to stick with him, it'll be worth my while. He's picking me up in about ten minutes."

"Where's he going to pick up the money?"

"He ain't told me that yet."

"If I were you I'd find something else to do this afternoon," Morales said.

"But if *I* were me, what would I do?"

"You *are* you, aren't you?"

"Damn right I am. A parolee trying to go straight, trying to do the right thing, but also trying to find some way to pay the bills. You tell me — what's the right thing to do?"

"What are you asking me?"

"Should I be letting them ill-gotten gains fall into the hands of an aider and abettor of perverts like McGrath?"

He could hear Morales laughing over the phone.

"In other words," Morales said, "would there be anything wrong with confiscating a pile of cash paid by a human-trafficking, child-abusing pimp to one of his accomplices for lying under oath?"

"Yeah," Ruffin said. "Anything wrong with that?"

At the division station Morales stuck two dollars in a vending machine for a lukewarm coffee on her way up to the office. Nobody knew where Burke was — probably at a bar or out sleeping in his car. Hague walked past Morales's desk without acknowledging her existence. He didn't seem to care if she came to work or not. He just wanted her to stop thinking about McGrath and Luisa Salazar. She decided to make another effort to talk to him. His office door was ajar and as she approached it she heard him on the phone.

"Plan C?" he asked whoever he was talking to. "How many letters of the alphabet are you gonna use up before you get this right?"

He listened on the phone for a while and then he said, "Okay, go ahead. Let that moron think he's getting a hundred grand." He listened a while longer and said, "Bank of America Plaza? That's where McGrath wants the drop?"

Where McGrath wants the drop?

"Is Chung on his way over there?"

Chung? On his way over there?

Holy shit.

Hague was involved in getting Chung's uncle's money to McGrath.

Morales slipped away from the door before Hague caught sight of her. She could hardly believe how stupid she had been.

Five miles away, the black Toyota Land Cruiser glided to a stop in a deserted parking lot behind the Sgarlatti food distribution warehouse near the Santa Monica Freeway. Less than a minute later a black and white LAPD van with two uniformed cops in the front seat — their names were Officers Harbison and Vigil — cruised in from the other side and parked facing the Land Cruiser.

Strausser and Duvaloy slipped out of the Land Cruiser and stood waiting beside it. Harbison and Vigil stayed in the LAPD van, engine running, windows rolled up.

Then the back door of the van opened and Detective Jerry Burke hoisted himself out into the moist sunlight. In his cheap suit and wrinkled shirt and drooping red tie, he looked like he'd spent the day sleeping in his clothes. The phone conversation with Hague was still ringing in his ears. "You let him get away the first time," Hague had said, "you and your pal Alonzo. Call that Plan A. And then yesterday with Dumb and Dumber — I mean Strausser and Duvaloy — that was supposed to be Plan B, the no screw-ups plan. What plan are you up to now? How many letters of the alphabet are you gonna use up before you get this right?"

Burke hated Hague almost as much as he hated Strausser and Duvaloy, the two morons who stood in front of him. They were the ones who'd put him in this position by not picking up McGrath and Ruffin the day before like they were supposed to. His voice brimmed with contempt as he repeated Hague's alphabetical analysis of the failures of the past few days. "Plan

A was what Alonzo Payne was supposed to do when the bus arrived," he said. "He screwed it up."

"Big time," Strausser agreed.

"Guy must be blind," Duvaloy added.

"Plan B was what you were supposed to do yesterday — grab McGrath and Ruffin together and take them out to the refinery — but you were so busy getting blowjobs you let them escape from the strip club."

"Human error," Strausser said.

"Shit happens," Duvaloy added.

"So this morning we shifted to Plan C. Chung's uncle owes McGrath fifty thousand dollars and now McGrath's upped it to a hundred. So the idea is, use that to set up a trap. Let McGrath think he's calling the shots, he'll bring Ruffin along as his bodyguard. Only he doesn't get the money because there isn't any money."

"Then grab them and take them out to the refinery," Strausser said. "Same as under Plan B."

"Melt them down into sludge," Duvaloy suggested.

"That was Plan C," Burke said. "Approved by Hague this morning. But now there's a new wrinkle, something we didn't see coming, something Hague still doesn't know about. Chung's uncle actually came up with the hundred grand. Apparently the son of a bitch keeps that kind of money in the fortune cookie jar. And he wants to make sure McGrath actually gets it. He insists that it be delivered by his fat nephew, who can't even walk without his oxygen tanks."

"So where does that put us?" Strausser asked.

"Plan D," Burke smiled. "It's a simple variation of Plan C. After Chung hands over the money and waddles home, we grab Ruffin and McGrath and take them out to the refinery. But — here's the good part — we keep the money."

Strausser and Duvaloy listened to the roar of the freeway blowing over them like a storm as they thought about Plan D. Strausser was the first to speak, his voice sounding ridiculously small coming from such a large man. "You think Chung's uncle will let us get away with that?"

"Chung's uncle gets what he bargained for, doesn't he?" Burke said. "What he wants is for McGrath to keep his mouth shut, and when we get done with McGrath his mouth will be done flapping forever. You can be sure of that. And we get the hundred grand."

"It's a win/win situation," Duvaloy observed.

"Hague's okay with this?" Strausser wanted to know.

"Hague thinks we're still on Plan C. He doesn't know there's any real money involved. And unless one of you douche bags spills the beans, he never will."

"How about the Commissioner?"

"It's the least that piece of shit can do for us," Burke said, "after what he's put us through."

"Amen to that," Duvaloy agreed.

"So then it's a three-way split?" Strausser asked hopefully.

"An even split," Burke smiled. "Half for me and half for the two of you. I want to be completely fair."

Morales stalked out of the division station, found her car in the parking lot and drove a few random blocks to clear her head. She asked herself over and over again if she could have misinterpreted what she'd overheard Hague saying on the phone: *Bank of America Plaza? That's where McGrath wants the drop? Is Chung on his way over there?* It could have meant that the payoff was a sting operation, run by the department or possibly the Feds, designed to entrap Chung and his uncle along with McGrath and expose the origin of McGrath's perjured testimony. Or the sting could have been targeted only at McGrath, with Chung (after all, he was a Corrections officer) baiting the hook for the police. But there was a more sinister explanation: that Hague was monitoring or even directing the payoff as part of the cover-up of what happened in that hotel room eight years before. In that event the payoff was probably a ruse to lure McGrath into a death trap, one of those shootings that happen every day when the wrong kind of person steps in front of a police gun barrel. And it would mean that Hague had always been part of the cover-up, that he'd reassigned Morales because she was sniffing too close to the truth. This must have gone on for years — until McGrath came back and threatened to talk. Then Hague had to act. The clueless and indifferent Burke posed no threat, but she, Morales, had to be put on ice before she knew too much.

And what about Ruffin? Was he being set up as collateral damage, a bystander to the payoff who'd be implicated or killed when the money drop scenario played out? She dialed Ruffin's number to warn him, but he wasn't answering. Probably because he'd already made up his mind to go along for the ride and steal the money from McGrath. Would it be a crime, he'd asked her, to confiscate a pile of money paid by a human-trafficking, child-abusing pimp to one of his accomplices for lying under oath? Maybe not, she could have told him if only he'd answer his phone.

But it might be last thing he ever did.

Kimberly sat in her van brooding about what she had to do that afternoon. She hated Chung, in his white linen suit and his short-brimmed Panama hat and the rolling oxygen tanks he had to push around wherever he went so his driver and bodyguard Felipe, that half-Chinese, half-Mexican freak, could keep both hands free in case he needed to shoot somebody. The two of them cruised around like a couple of beauty queens in a 1990s vintage Lincoln Town Car, white with white leather interior and a white vinyl top. In a few minutes they'd come back from Chung's uncle's with the $100,000 McGrath had demanded for keeping his mouth shut. If there was anybody she hated more than Chung, it was McGrath, for what she'd had to put up with from that pig in the past two days. It went with the territory, she told herself — which was why, when this was all over with, she planned to light out for a different territory. Someplace like Fiji or Tahiti where she could invest in real estate, maybe open a souvenir shop selling worthless crap to tourists. She'd already decided to steal the $100,000 before it ever got into McGrath's filthy paws.

"The money has to be in a blue United Airlines satchel," she'd told Chung. "One of those flight bags. McGrath insisted on that."

"It's got to be in that exact kind of satchel?" Chung asked. "Why?"

"The guy's an asswipe. What can I say?"

Chung thought it over and decided to comply. "Okay, I have one at home," he said. "I'll take it to my uncle's and we'll put the money in it and come back here in the Town Car and pick you up. Say about 4:30?"

"I'll be waiting."

What she didn't mention was that she also had a blue United Airlines flight bag that probably looked just like the one Chung planned to put the money in, or close enough that she could switch the two before they arrived at Bank of America Plaza. Felipe would be driving and Chung would be fiddling with his oxygen tanks, especially if she lit a cigarette inside the car. Making the switch would be a piece of cake.

She stuck her empty satchel in a white plastic bag and planned her itinerary to the South Seas while she waited for Chung and Felipe to pick her up.

23

What happened next is a little confusing — if you think in terms of people.

Ruffin, McGrath, Morales, Kimberly, Chung, Jayden, Shanise, Derek, Alonzo, Burke, Strausser, Duvaloy, Olaf the Pool Boy — if you look at things from their individual points of view, what you see might seem sort of random, even chaotic. But remember, this is L.A. Five or six million people rushing around all day long doing things that are crazy or illegal or downright stupid. Random is as good as it gets. The idea of order in L.A. is chaos repeated so many times that it looks like a pattern. Like the eternal traffic jam that forms the backbone of the city. Nobody intended it but it goes on forever, the only human artifact visible from outer space.

Before you can even think about the people in that traffic jam, you have to find their vehicles. In L.A. it's all about cars. That afternoon, if you could have picked out the individual cars, these would have been the ones to watch:

A battered 1980s Cadillac, sea-green, two-door.

A red F-150 pickup.

A black BMW with tinted windows.

A white Lincoln Town Car with a white vinyl roof.

A black and white LAPD van.

A Toyota Land Cruiser, black.

A silver Maserati convertible with the top down.

All lurching forward through the rush-hour traffic at a desperate snail's pace as they converged on Bank of America Plaza.

There were men in those cars, and a boy, and a woman, each with his or her own destiny. One of the men — McGrath — hoped to get $100,000 and flee to Belize. Several others planned to steal that money from McGrath. The boy intended to shoot Ruffin with a .45-caliber Glock 21 at close range.

Burke had promised his boss that Ruffin and McGrath and Alonzo Payne would all be dead by the end of the day.

It was almost five o'clock.

24

On Wilshire Boulevard, McGrath swerved across two lanes of traffic, daring the commuters in their fancy cars to broadside the Cadillac and knock themselves out on their airbags. None took the dare. Instead they screeched to a stop and gave him plenty of space to pick up Ruffin and take off gurgling and fuming toward the downtown skyscrapers. Ruffin glanced at the dashboard clock — ten minutes to five. Country music wailed out mercilessly from the radio.

"I stopped by the sister's house," McGrath said, "and guess who was there? The goddam sister. Just as hot in person as she was in that picture."

"Did you kill her?" Ruffin asked him.

"Hell no. I asked her to marry me."

"What'd you do a thing like that for?"

"She was holding a gun to my head," McGrath said. "Twelve gauge pump action Remington. It was either fork over eighty percent now, or marry her and wait for the divorce."

"Yeah, but eighty percent?"

"This is L.A.," McGrath said. "You do what you got to do to stay in one piece."

The traffic was getting ugly as rush hour locked in. McGrath drove through it like a rodeo cowboy breaking a steer — bucking and weaving, waving his arms, honking his horn. Yelling at the other drivers:

"Watch out, you piece of shit!"

"Do that again and I'll cut your goddam nuts off!"

"Blow it out your ass, shitsucker!"

Ruffin switched off the radio. "Where are we going, anyway?" he asked.

"I told Kimberly I'd pick her up," McGrath said. "She's doing some banking downtown."

"Banking? Whores got banking?"

"Whores practically invented banking," McGrath said. "Where do you think all the money comes from?"

Jayden had come home from school to grab a bite and change his clothes. He'd be going back out soon, dressed to the nines in his gang regalia and a gray hoodie. That's what he always wore when he went back out. He always used the back door.

Derek watched the back of the house from the garage. He'd gathered some equipment — ropes, knives, a black mask, night vision goggles — from his days as a Marine commando and stashed it under the front seat of his F-150 pickup. He wore a black jumpsuit and black boots and a black knit cap. He checked and loaded a 9-mm SIG Sauer semi-automatic pistol and deposited that, along with an extra ammunition clip, in the glove compartment. He had a license to carry — there were some neighborhoods where he wouldn't make FedEx deliveries without a firearm. He was an expert marksman, though a little rusty. Hadn't been to the firing range for over a year.

Derek didn't miss the Marines, but he missed the sensation of power and importance he'd experienced in the service, especially in those tense, excruciating moments in Afghanistan when his life and the lives of his comrades hung in the balance. Such moments didn't come often driving a FedEx truck. He'd tried to domesticate himself by marrying Shanise and playing dad to Jayden, but that hadn't worked out so well. Shanise always put her son first — that was natural, though often exasperating. Derek hadn't foreseen the problems Jayden would bring to the marriage. In the past couple of years, whenever Derek tried to assert himself — for the boy's own good — Jayden had just brushed him off like an annoying insect. Now things had suddenly gone serious. It wasn't a question of making him do his homework or clean his room, the kid was flirting with disaster and didn't even seem to know it. Derek's emotions ranged between anger and despair, with occasional lapses into cynical indifference. Sometimes he just wanted to beat the hell out of the kid, and out of Shanise too for coddling him when she should have been supporting him in his efforts to discipline the boy. What would she say if she knew what he was doing now? Lying in wait for Jayden in the garage so he could follow him out and try to catch him in the act so he could talk — or maybe beat — some sense into him. What would Shanise say about that?

Derek peered through the small window in the garage door as Jayden slipped out of the house and headed toward the street. When the boy was out of sight, he climbed into the F-150 and glided out of the driveway, then crept along the street until he saw Jayden strutting down the sidewalk ahead of him.

Alonzo's black BMW pulled up and stopped beside Jayden, picked him up, and headed downtown.

Derek eased out in the F-150 and followed at a distance.

Alonzo piloted the BMW toward the downtown skyscrap-crs through the thickening traffic. "This your lucky day, Jayden," he said. "The man call and give us another chance."

"What man?"

Alonzo laughed. *The* man. That's what man. *The* man. You don't want to know his name."

He reached over and handed Jayden a gun. It was a .45-caliber Glock 21. It felt surprisingly heavy and cold but Jayden tried to seem indifferent.

"This the hit you spoke up for," Alonzo said. "You still in, right?"

"Sure. Just like I said."

"It's set up for six o'clock," Alonzo said. "At one of them big bank plazas downtown."

"Downtown?"

"The more people around, the better," Alonzo said. "When you finish you just drop the piece and get out of there."

"You gonna be there?"

"Sure, I'll be right behind you. You do just what I say. Might be some last minute changes. I don't trust that bitch."

"What bitch?"

"The one that set this up. But he don't know you, so you got nothing to worry about. Just don't take that piece out till I tell you to, hear? Do exactly what I tell you."

"Okay."

"You ever use one of them?"

"Sure, plenty of times."

Alonzo smiled. He knew Jayden was lying but he pretended to believe him. It would be easier to keep him in line with a fake identity he had to live up to. "There's gonna be another guy there with him," he said. "I give you the word, you waste him too."

Jayden stared out the window, where the world sped by in slow motion. He felt a little sick.

It was after 5:30 and motion had all but ceased on Wilshire Boulevard and surrounding streets. The cars just twitched in place like flies stuck on flypaper. McGrath navigated with frenzied slowness, jumping his brakes, jostling ahead in fits and starts, shouting out the window at the other drivers:

"Go ahead, make my day, douche bag!"

"Bite me, pissant!"

Ruffin stayed calm. "I been thinking about what you said this morning," he told McGrath. "About how nasty the kids are today."

"It's scary," McGrath said, shaking his head.

"Maybe us older guys need to set an example."

"Set an example? An example of what?"

"Not being an asshole."

McGrath slammed on his brakes and screamed at a white-haired old lady in a Mercedes: "Learn to drive, bitch!" Then he turned his head around to look at Ruffin. "What are you talking about?"

"You know," Ruffin said. "Showing them the right way to act."

McGrath laughed. "What are you, a Young Republican? Showing them the right way to act! Next thing you'll be out looking for a job."

"I might do that if it meant I could see my boy," Ruffin said.

McGrath tossed his cigarette out the window. "How the mighty have fallen."

"You ever had a job?"

"I applied for one once, but the psychologist called me a lyin' sociopath."

"People got no respect," Ruffin said.

"Yeah," McGrath agreed. "I might go back and strangle that son of a bitch." He rammed his front bumper against a Honda Civic that tried to cut in front of him and nudged it out of the way. "Nobody calls me a liar."

Derek felt grateful for the rush hour traffic tie-up. It meant he could keep the black BMW in sight without being too conspicuous in his red F-150. He took out his phone and dialed Shanise, who was just leaving work.

"I'm following Jayden in that gangster's BMW," he told her. "They're headed downtown, I don't know why."

"What are you going to do when you catch up to them?" she asked.

"That depends on what they're doing," Derek said. "If it's something dangerous or illegal, I'm going to get Jayden out of there if I have to drag him by the ears."

"I think you should go home and calm down. We don't need any heroics. This isn't Afghanistan."

"No, it's L.A., and that's a helluva lot worse."

Shanise was in tears. "Tell me you didn't bring any guns with you," she said.

"Shanise, I know what I'm doing," he said. "If you want to do something useful, why don't you try to call him?"

"What good's that going to do?"

"Just to let him know we're watching. That's important to a kid, just to know somebody's watching."

Jayden's phone played a hip hop ring tone and he pulled it out to answer. "This is my mama," he told Alonzo.

"When you with me, you don't got a mama," Alonzo said.

Jayden turned off the sound without answering.

"You better ditch that phone," Alonzo said. "They can track you with the GPS."

"I turned it off."

Alonzo snatched the phone out of Jayden's hand, crushed it under his foot and tossed it out the window. "You do what I tell you," he said. "Got that?"

Felipe piloted the Lincoln Town Car as if it were a Boeing 747 gliding toward its destination without a cloud in the sky. Kimberly sat in the back seat with Chung and his oxygen tanks and the blue United Airlines flight bag full of money, which he clutched with both hands at the place where his lap would have been if he'd had a lap. She had her own matching satchel, stuffed with bundles of cut-up newspaper, inside a white plastic bag so he wouldn't see it before she made the switch, but she hadn't counted on being blocked by the oxygen tanks. They occupied the space between her and Chung with their plastic tubes curling toward his nose. There was no way she could reach across the tanks to Chung's satchel without entangling her hand in the tubes, especially with Felipe watching in the rear view mirror. As the car leaned around a corner, she managed inconspicuously to turn down the oxygen level in the hope that Chung would suffocate or at least fall asleep long enough for her to switch the satchels.

A black and white LAPD van, lights flashing, wove its way through the traffic near Bank of America Plaza. Two uniformed cops sat in the front seat, Harbison the driver, Vigil beside him. Burke sat behind them in the back seat. "Go around this corner and into the underground parking garage," Burke said. "Turn the van around and park near the ramp on the first level down."

He pulled out his phone and dialed Strausser. Strausser and Duvaloy were driving separately in the Toyota Land Cruiser.

"Where the hell are you?" Burke demanded.

"We're stuck in traffic," Strausser said. "It's a lot worse than we expected."

"You didn't know there'd be traffic in L.A. at 5:30 in the afternoon?"

"Like I said, it's worse than usual."

"Don't screw it up this time, Strausser. This is your last chance to get this right."

The traffic on Wilshire Boulevard finally sent McGrath over the edge. When a UPS truck blocked an intersection, McGrath drove the Cadillac up on the sidewalk to get around it. Pedestrians scattered in all directions as he honked his way back onto the street.

"What's the hurry?" Ruffin said. "You gonna get us killed."

McGrath still hadn't told Ruffin the real reason they were driving downtown. "I told Kimberly I'd pick her up at the bank at six o'clock," he said.

"You told some whore you met yesterday you'd pick her up at six o'clock, so we gotta get killed on the way over there?"

"You know why you'll never make it on the outside, Ruffin?" McGrath said. "You got a bad attitude. Punctuality is one of the most important ways you show respect for others."

A charcoal gray Audi A8 veered in front of them. McGrath slammed on the brakes and leaned on his horn. "Get out of my way, you worthless sack of shit!"

They finally reached the entrance to the underground parking garage at Bank of America Plaza. The Cadillac, Alonzo's BMW, and Derek's pickup arrived separately, one after the other, and drove down the ramp into the garage. McGrath parked the Cadillac on Level One in sight of the police van, which was parked near the ramp with nobody in it. Strausser's Land Cruiser, looking like every other SUV in the garage, stood empty beside the police van. Alonzo's BMW and Derek's red pickup continued down to Level Two.

McGrath jumped out of the Cadillac but Ruffin stayed in his seat. As usual, McGrath left the keys in the ignition.

"Hey, what are you waiting for?" McGrath asked.

"I got such a bad attitude," Ruffin said, "you can go meet Kimberly by yourself."

"I was just busting your balls, Ruffin. You got a great attitude."

"Up your ass."

"See what I mean? That's what I call a great attitude."

Morales's red Ford Focus wasn't part of the traffic jam converging on Bank of America Plaza. She sat in the same bar she'd visited the night before, Antonito's, wondering if anyone would pay any attention to her. No one did, not the hardhats or the suits or even the bartender, who walked past about ten times before taking her order. Were they all that afraid of a woman who might look a little hard to handle? Or could they somehow tell she was a cop? She ordered a Moscow mule, in honor of the elusive Russian strangler. Had any such man really existed? Brian Epstein, the Assistant D.A., thought not; the only one who'd seen the Russian was McGrath, who was obviously lying. Then who was the strangler? Not McGrath himself — even Ruffin had rejected that suggestion — or Chung's aging uncle, or Chung, who would have passed out from the effort. And the most gnawing question of all: How was this troubling cold case related to the shooting of Luisa Salazar and her mother? Could they — really the mother, since Luisa hadn't been born yet — have been somehow involved in what happened in Chung's uncle's hotel eight years ago? Was the mother a witness who'd come back to testify? And another thing: What was the connection between all these things — Luisa, Luisa's mother, McGrath, the strangler, Hague, the cover-up, the payoff — with Kenny Ruffin? Was it just a coincidence that Ruffin rode back from San Quentin on the same bus as Cat McGrath?

She dialed Ruffin again. Still no answer. Not even a cue to leave a voice message. She wondered if he'd already made his move and was busy disappearing with McGrath's money. She wondered if she'd ever see him again.

She dialed Burke. No answer.

There was too much to think about. Time for another drink. Those Moscow mules weren't half bad.

In the back seat of the Lincoln Town Car, Kimberly waited for the lowered oxygen level to take effect. After ten minutes of bobbing and swaying, Chung started to look groggy. He drooled, his head dipped forward, and a few seconds later he fell asleep. Kimberly was able to reach past the oxygen tubes and switch the satchels just before Felipe brought the car to a landing in a parking lot about a block from Bank of America Plaza. Before he killed the engine she set the oxygen level back up to where it had been.

Chung woke up but didn't notice that the bags had been switched. Kimberly helped Felipe extricate Chung and his oxygen tanks from the back seat.

"We won't be needing this," Felipe said, prying the fake satchel away from Chung and tossing it back into the car.

He reached into Kimberly's plastic bag and removed the satchel she had hidden there. "Let's take the one with the money in it."

His eyes told her that she'd be hearing more about this later.

On Level Two of the parking garage, Alonzo and Jayden climbed out of the BMW and walked toward the stairs. Jayden fingered the Glock in his pocket and kept his eyes fixed straight ahead of him. Derek watched from his pickup, which he'd parked where they couldn't see it.

"You stay ahead of me," Alonzo told Jayden. "This your hit, not mine. But you keep your eye on me and do just what I say, hear? Keep that piece in your pocket 'til I tell you to take it out."

25

Bank of America Plaza is an artificial landscape of concrete and marble, trees, ponds and waterfalls built around the skyscraper featured in the 1970s disaster movie, *The Towering Inferno*. Next to the main entrance stands a monolith of twisted orange girders, apparently left over from the fire (official sources identify it as a famous sculpture by Alexander Calder). To McGrath it was a set of golden arches undoubtedly marking the presence of a McDonalds franchise, which was why he chose it as the site of his rendezvous with Kimberly. Under those rainbow-like arches he hoped to find the treasure that would fulfill the dreams of a lifetime.

He and Ruffin took up their positions under the golden arches a little before six o'clock. Office and hotel towers loomed on all sides, casting shadows over the crowded streets and sidewalks. The bank plaza surged with employees leaving work, teenagers, young lovers, vendors, buskers, tourists and street people. Across from the golden arches, a garden with trees, ponds, and concrete pathways stretched along West 4th and continued back around the skyscraper to South Hope. Strausser and Duvaloy loitered under a tree in the garden, keeping careful watch on the main entrance. Officers Harbison and Vigil — the uniformed cops who'd arrived in the LAPD van — stood half-concealed in the lobby, focusing their attention on the two ex-cons passing their time under the sculpture. A hippie twanging a guitar croaked out lyrics nobody cared to understand.

From a raised ledge that gave him a bird's-eye view of the plaza, Detective Jerry Burke surveyed the scene through his iPhone. With the aid of a binoculars app, he could follow every move that McGrath and Ruffin made, every change of expression, every flick of the wrist. He could practically read their lips. Through the mike on his phone, he could stay in voice contact with Strausser and Duvaloy and the two uniformed cops, directing them as the situation developed. He appeared calm and cold-blooded but his clothes were soaked with nervous sweat. This was the most important operation he'd ever been entrusted him with. The idea was to grab McGrath and Ruffin together so they could be disposed of together, out at the old Jackson Oil refinery near Long Beach. Alonzo had been invited too, so that worthless piece of shit could be dissolved in the same sludge pit as the others. It wasn't as if Burke enjoyed this sort of thing. He was no ethical paragon, but given his druthers he would have been home watching a ball game. He was only following orders — even Hague himself was only following orders. If you looked into things deeply enough, even the Commissioner was probably just following orders. It was wheels within wheels, and you didn't want to know where the top wheel was spinning. The department had to be protected or they would all go down, the whole city could go down. And for Burke and Strausser and Duvaloy (though not for Hague, who still didn't know about it) there was an extra added incentive: the $100,000 in cash Chung would be bringing in a blue United Airlines flight bag, which, if all went according to plan, McGrath would never lay his hands on.

Lounging inconspicuously on a wooden bench beside an iron fence, Olaf the Pool Boy watched McGrath and Ruffin chatting under the golden arches. They looked like a couple of ex-cons, barely back on the street and hardly worth the risk of taking out in such a public place. Back in Minnesota he wouldn't have risked it — he would have followed them out of town and left them bleeding out in a snowdrift along the road. But life has its trade-offs. In Minnesota you can't get a great tan, spend your days hanging out by the pool, or take yoga classes on the beach. And business is business wherever you go. If Bob said take them out in broad daylight in Bank of America Plaza, that's what he had to do. The tradeoff was he got to drive over there in a Maserati convertible and he didn't have to stay in his cabana all night while Bob and Joanne played with their bratty grandchildren.

When Ruffin and McGrath turned around to stare at something, Olaf looked in that direction and spied Chung, flanked by Felipe and Kimberly, pushing his oxygen tank in snail-like paces across the plaza. The satchel full of money was in his hands.

Olaf held his phone to his ear, describing what he saw and receiving real-time instructions from Bob Waterson. "The place is crawling with cops," he told Bob.

"Let me guess," Bob said. "There's Detective Burke, plain clothes, probably off to one side issuing orders on his phone — he's in charge of the rest of them. Then a couple of uniforms lurking inside the bank lobby, probably a few plainclothes cops trying to blend into the crowd. The money will be carried to McGrath by a fat Chinese guy in a white linen suit. That's Chung. We insisted that he bring the money so we'd know exactly where it was at all times."

"I see him," Olaf said. "He moves in slow motion."

"Probably pushing his oxygen tanks. He's got COPD. Is he carrying the money?"

"Looks like it. He's carrying something anyway."

"Anybody with him?"

"Yeah, a big Asian dude and a blonde who looks like a hooker."

"What's she doing there?"

"She's pushing the oxygen tanks on a cart."

There was a pause while Bob considered the situation. "Okay, here's what I want you to do," he said. "When Chung gets about twenty-five feet from McGrath, pull out your piece — what have you got on you?"

"Nine millimeter Heckler & Koch."

"Good. You don't have a silencer on it, do you?"

"Not yet."

"OK, leave it off. When Chung gets close enough pull out your piece and fire a couple of shots in the air. Everybody will hit the ground, including all the cops. Stash it back in your pocket and grab the money from Chung and run into the garage. If McGrath and Ruffin follow you — which they probably will — take them out."

"What if the cops follow me?"

"Keep running. They're probably after the money too."

McGrath was alert, fearing a trap. He thought Ruffin was there to protect him. He didn't know that Ruffin was one of the people he needed to be worried about.

"This ain't no McDonalds," Ruffin said.

"Them arches sort of look like a rainbow, don't they? Maybe this is where I'll find my pot of gold."

"What's this money you keep talking about?" Ruffin asked. "Why does Chung's uncle owe you money?"

"That's something you're better off not knowing," McGrath said. "I don't want to see you get hurt they way they hurt me." He peered into Ruffin's eyes with the most sincere expression he knew how to fake. "I hope you don't mind me saying so, but I consider you a friend."

Ruffin raised his eyebrows. "You got friends?"

"Sure, I got friends. I got friends in every jail in the West, even a few on death row. Let me tell you, it takes twenty years to life to build up friendships like that."

McGrath kept his eyes on Kimberly on the opposite side of the plaza. She trudged slowly between Chung and Felipe, pushing Chung's rolling oxygen tanks. Felipe had his huge paw fastened around her arm and she didn't look happy. Gasping for breath, Chung clutched the blue satchel full of money in both hands.

The three of them stopped every two steps so that Chung could catch his breath. Their progress across the plaza was excruciatingly slow, even slower than the pace of the traffic on

Wilshire Boulevard. There was something unearthly in that slowness. Ruffin sensed danger.

"When I get my money," McGrath said, "I'm going down to Belize and do some fishing. They got tarpon down there about six feet long. You like fishing, maybe you could come along if you want to."

"Thanks but I got shit to do," Ruffin said, looking away.

"What kind of shit?"

"Maybe start a business," Ruffin said. "A rib joint or something."

"Where you gonna get the money to do that?"

With Kimberly, Chung and Felipe within sixty feet of the arches, Burke muttered an order into his phone. Harbison and Vigil slipped out of the building through the revolving door and began to close in behind Ruffin and McGrath.

Jayden and Alonzo edged around a corner and glided toward the golden arches. Jayden wore a gray hoodie pulled up around his head. Derek trailed behind them, keeping out of sight. Alonzo saw the two cops moving toward the arches and stopped in his tracks.

Jayden walked on ahead.

"I'm working on getting the money for the rib joint," Ruffin said, keeping his eyes on Chung's blue flight bag. "Could be getting it real soon."

"You let me know when your rib joint opens," McGrath said. "I'll be your first customer."

"I'm thinking you'll be my first investor," Ruffin said.

Duvaloy and Strausser, following Burke's instructions, moved toward Alonzo. They didn't notice Jayden, who plunged ahead without looking back. If they'd seen him it wouldn't have mattered. They didn't know who Jayden was.

"Hey Jayden," Alonzo said. "Hold up! Hold up, I said!" His voice was drowned out by the hippie guitarist and an airplane passing overhead.

Jayden didn't hear Alonzo, or if he did, he paid no attention. He pressed forward through the crowd, eyes fixed on Ruffin. He had the gun in his hand.

"Jayden! Stop!"

Strausser heard Alonzo's voice and turned toward the kid he was shouting at, who marched forward like a sleepwalker.

Burke couldn't believe what he saw happening. His eyes darted from the screen on his phone to the plaza and back to the phone. McGrath and Ruffin appeared on the screen as big as life, talking and joking, oblivious to the approaching threat. Burke turned his phone toward the kid in the hoodie, who was making a beeline toward Ruffin. He held what appeared to be a Glock 21, a .45-caliber semi-automatic which had been banned for use by the LAPD. It was too unreliable, too hard to control. Too dangerous.

The kid raised the gun in both hands and started firing, spraying bullets in front of him, out of control. Shattering plate glass windows, ricocheting off the sculpture and the marble facade. Explosions echoed between the skyscrapers like armies exchanging fire.

Pandemonium took over the plaza, people screaming and running in all directions. Throwing themselves down on the pavement, behind trees in the park, into the ponds. Trying to escape, trying to protect each other. Crying. Praying. Passing out.

Chung was one of those who passed out, collapsing into a shapeless heap. Kimberly and Felipe left him where he fell and ran back the way they came. The four cops — Duvaloy, Strausser, Harbison and Vigil — all ducked for cover.

Ruffin and McGrath were down, flat on the granite pavement under the arches like a couple of squashed bugs. Had they been hit? Burke couldn't tell — there were too many people dodging around them, frantic to escape. If any of those .45 slugs hit them — it didn't matter where — they were dead. Where was the kid who did the shooting?

Burke didn't see Jayden, who'd dropped the gun and fled into the crowd. But he recognized Alonzo standing where he had stopped.

When Burke looked back under the arches, he couldn't find Ruffin, who'd apparently risen from the dead. McGrath was still down, but not for long. Harbison and Vigil pounced on him and hauled him up trembling from the pavement, handcuffed him behind his back, and dragged him toward the parking garage. Apparently he hadn't been hit.

Strausser and Duvaloy chased after the kid in the hoodie, cornered him against an iron fence. Even in the noise and confusion Burke could hear them shout, "Police officers! Stop!" They wrestled him down and snapped him in cuffs and bounced his head against the pavement a couple of times to keep him quiet.

Where was Ruffin? Now Burke saw him, running with something in his hand toward Alonzo, who sprang away from him toward the garage. Ruffin ran after him.

It was all over in about thirty seconds.

There were a couple of things Burke hadn't noticed.

He hadn't noticed Derek frozen in panic at the edge of the plaza. Derek had fought in Afghanistan but nothing in that experience had prepared him for what he'd just seen: Jayden going berserk with a semi-automatic, trying to kill his own father. Strausser and Duvaloy charging after him, wrestling him down, twisting his wrists into handcuffs and banging his head on the cement. Derek couldn't move a muscle.

And he hadn't noticed Ruffin jumping up under the arches and swerving through the frenzied crowd to where Chung lay on the pavement, snatching the blue United Airlines flight bag out of his hands as Felipe and Kimberly ran away — or that other guy, the suntanned blond guy who also tried to grab the money, who Ruffin punched and pushed aside and kicked in the head before he ran into the garage.

26

When Ruffin stood up under the arches he didn't know if he was dead or alive. He checked for bullet holes, for blood, for pain, and there weren't any. The crowd scattering around him gave him a sensation of power, that he could walk away unscathed and unseen. There was Chung sprawled on the pavement hanging onto that blue satchel. The whole picture had suddenly come into focus: McGrath waiting for Kimberly, Kimberly arriving with Chung, Chung bringing a satchel that must have held the money his uncle owed McGrath. Ruffin ran to scoop it up and a big blond guy tried to grab the satchel and Ruffin had to punch him and knock him to the pavement and kick him in the head for good measure, and then he saw Alonzo glaring back at him from near the bank tower. Alonzo'd been trying to kill him ever since he got back from Quentin. But he didn't shoot at him this time: Ruffin had seen the shooter, it was some kid in a hoodie who must have been in Alonzo's gang. Ruffin leaped after Alonzo who fled into the parking garage. Ruffin wanted to kill him but at the same time he told himself to stop. He had the money in that flight bag, more money than he'd ever dreamed of. He had everything he needed to go somewhere and start a new life. The L.A. cops hated him, Shanise didn't want him back, wouldn't even let him see Jayden. His friends were all dead or in jail or living under a freeway overpass. There was no place for him here. He could go to the islands, Jamaica or someplace, and live like a king. Open his rib joint, send money back to Jayden and Shanise, never think about McGrath again for the rest of his life. But before he disappeared he needed to know who Alonzo was working for and why he wanted to kill him.

Inside the garage he lost sight of Alonzo, but he could hear him tramping toward the ramp that led up to the street. He followed the pounding and saw Alonzo near the bottom of the ramp, stopped by the sight of the police van parked there, afraid to go any farther. He ducked out of sight behind some parked cars and Ruffin followed him into the shadows, cornering him behind a dumpster.

Ruffin dropped the satchel and threw himself on Alonzo, wrapping his hands around his throat, crushing him against a concrete wall. "Why you trying to kill me?" he shouted, tightening his grip.

"Payback for yesterday at Wellingtons," Alonzo smirked, trying to preserve his attitude—arrogant, a little sly, like he had some power over Ruffin.

"Bullshit," Ruffin said. "You been trying to kill me since I got back to L.A."

"It ain't you I been after," Alonzo said. "It's that peckerwood you go around with. McGrath."

Ruffin could hardly believe what he'd just heard. He squinted at Alonzo to see if this was more bullshit. "All this time you been trying to kill McGrath?"

"That's right," Alonzo gloated. "Shoot him getting off the bus. Shoot him in the emergency room. Shoot him in the taxi. You so stupid you keep getting in the way. It's him I been trying to kill."

"That lying bastard!"

"Maybe you his duck decoy," Alonzo smiled. "Maybe you his bullet-proof shield. Maybe you just his bitch."

Ruffin hurled Alonzo against the wall and almost strangled him.

"Yo, I'm just the messenger!" Alonzo gasped.

"Does McGrath know you're trying to kill him?"

"Never been no mistake about that. That why he keeps you around for protection."

"I'll kill him myself," Ruffin said.

"Too late for that," Alonzo said. "The cops got him now, but they ain't taking him to no police station. He a dead man."

"What you talking about?"

"Who you think told me to shoot that fool in the first place? Damn white cop name of Burke busted me with guns in my car and told me what I had to do. The cops want that man dead."

Ruffin tightened his grip around Alonzo's throat. "I'm gonna kill you anyway."

Alonzo smiled like he thought he held all the cards. "You kill me you won't find out something else you need to know," he said. "Something you need to know real bad."

Ruffin shoved him harder against the wall. "You tell me what it is and I'll think about letting you live."

"You gotta do more than just think about it."

"OK, what is it?"

"That kid that just took those shots at you?" Alonzo said. "That be your son Jayden."

Ruffin felt like exploding. He slammed Alonzo against the wall and left him in a heap as he grabbed the satchel and ran back to his car.

He unlocked the trunk and tossed the blue satchel on top of the Molotov cocktails. As he stepped back toward the driver's door he saw Burke charging across the parking area. He crouched next to the car as Burke went past him toward the ramp. When he peered around behind Burke he was surprised at what he saw. Burke didn't go to the police van but stopped and stood still, listening. Then he threaded his way between the parked cars toward the dumpster where Ruffin had just left Alonzo. Ruffin decided to follow him there. He was still seething with anger at what Alonzo had told him. He hoped he would find out it wasn't true.

He sneaked up by the dumpster where he could hear Burke and Alonzo talking. It wasn't a friendly conversation. Burke had Alonzo pinned in the corner and Alonzo looked scared to death. "You dumb shit," Burke said. "You weren't supposed to shoot unless I told you to."

"I didn't shoot," Alonzo mumbled. He couldn't talk because Burke held something pressed against his throat. "It was that kid who done it."

"I told you to come alone."

"You know who that kid is?"

"I don't give a shit," Burke said. "Why did you bring him along?"

"That's Ruffin's kid Jayden."

"Ruffin's kid?"

"He said he wanted to kill that man," Alonzo said. "He don't know who it is."

"I still don't get why you brought him along."

"I had a feeling you was setting me up to get shot."

"Guess again," Burke said. He slashed whatever he held in his hand — it must have been a knife or a razor blade — across Alonzo's throat. Blood spurted out and Alonzo slumped to the floor.

Ruffin ducked behind a Chevy Suburban until Burke was out of sight. Then he threaded his way back until he could see the police van parked at the bottom of the ramp. McGrath stood there, head down, handcuffed behind his back — Harbison and Vigil were shoving him into the back seat. Kimberly was there too — they put her in beside McGrath and slammed the door. Then Duvaloy and Strausser tripped down the ramp dragging Jayden in handcuffs. They opened the tailgate door and shoved him inside the van.

Ruffin felt on fire, ready to explode. In his imagination he raced to the Cadillac, to the tire iron under the front seat and the Molotov cocktails in the trunk. Did he have time to use them? He saw now that those two thugs who'd been tailing him in the Land Cruiser were cops — dirty cops, like Morales said — and they were taking Jayden and McGrath somewhere to kill them. He'd just watched Burke kill Alonzo the way you'd swat a bug. That's what they were going to do to Jayden. There was no possibility of running now, no escape to the islands with his bag full of money. He still couldn't believe what Alonzo'd told him about Jayden, though he knew it was true, because Alonzo said the same thing to Burke. His own son had tried to kill him. Why? It didn't matter. He had to save him.

When the van raced up the ramp, Ruffin ran back to the Cadillac and jumped in. No matter what happened, he had to catch up with that van. And if he ever saw Burke again he would stomp him into a thousand pieces.

27

Dawdling over her last Moscow mule, Morales asked herself why she was getting so involved with Ruffin. Driving him out to the homeless camp, changing his bandage, recruiting him to investigate the police, even tacitly encouraging his crazy scheme to steal McGrath's payoff money. Why didn't she just let him go his own way? It must have been some kind of rebellion against the phony male-dominated world she lived in, in theory so masculine and strong, in reality epitomized by the pathetic, patronizing eunuchs she had to deal with every day, from Hague and Burke to this pitiful row of losers lining the bar in Antonito's, who whispered about her to each other but didn't have the balls to look her in the eye. Ruffin represented everything they hated and feared because they knew they could never measure up to it. They couldn't allow his kind of man to exist in their cramped, twisted, treacherous world. What did Morales see in him? He was a criminal, a violent gang leader, but she trusted him. He was the one man she wasn't afraid of. Did he have any idea what he was up against? Surprisingly, he seemed naive, almost innocent by today's standards. It was as if he'd been on a desert island for the past seventeen years. He'd learned the horrors of prison but missed the degradation of politics, the criminalization of business, the corporatization of crime. Morales feared for his life.

The police van, lights flashing, navigated through the traffic with the Cadillac jockeying unnoticed behind it. They were headed south toward Long Beach on the 110. On their right the sun was setting into thick clouds over the Pacific Ocean. It was going to be a dark night.

Harbison dialed his phone and Burke answered. "Yeah?"

"We're on our way out there," Harbison said.

Burke stood behind a pillar in the parking garage, wiping Alonzo's blood off his hands with a handkerchief. "Do you have the money?" he asked.

"Somebody must have picked it up," Harbison said.

"You stupid shits. Did you get Ruffin?"

"He got away but we'll find him," Harbison said.

"How are you going to find Ruffin?"

"Don't worry, we'll find him."

"I'll tell you how," Burke said. "You've got the kid, right? The kid that did the shooting? You know who that kid is? That's Ruffin's kid."

Harbison laughed out loud. "Ruffin's kid was trying to kill him?"

"That's right."

"I've got to hand it to you, Burke. You cover all the bases."

"Alonzo deserves the credit for that one."

"What do you want us to do with McGrath?"

"Don't do anything with him," Burke said, "until I get there." He hated McGrath almost as much as he'd hated Alonzo and he looked forward to his demise. "And you better find that money or you'll be swimming in the same sludge pond as McGrath."

Burke hung up and dialed Hague. "We've got McGrath," he told him. "Ruffin got away."

"How the hell did that happen?"

"It's temporary. We've got something he wants."

Hague didn't probe for the details. "What about your friend Alonzo?"

"Unfortunately Ruffin slit his throat in the parking garage. He died before we could call an ambulance."

"Such a shame," Hague said. "What about Morales?"

"Something tells me she's in danger too," Burke said. "You want me to call her?"

"No, let me do that. I owe her a call."

Hague needed some time to think before he called Morales. He liked her, admired her, even had fantasies about her sometimes, but everybody in the division knew she was trouble. Stubborn, too inquisitive, a little too sympathetic to the criminal element, as you'd expect for someone with her background who pulled political strings to get where she was, and let's face it she'd played the woman card a few too many times to be trusted. Nobody's perfect, everybody had their weaknesses but hers weren't the same ones everybody else had — she didn't seem to care how the department looked in the media, for instance — and that put her in danger, like Burke said. The question Hague needed to answer was: How much did she know? She'd been snooping around but did she really know anything? If she did, well — he'd cross that bridge when he came to it. The first step was to get her on the phone. He dialed her cell number.

"Morales?" he said when she answered. "Where were you today?"

"I was in the office," she said. "Didn't you see me?"

"I've been pretty busy," Hague said. "You know, with this and that. I guess I missed you."

"I've been busy too," she said.

"Oh?"

"I think I know why they're targeting McGrath. It goes back to that human trafficking case he was involved in."

Hague was coming to the decision point he'd been trying to avoid. He took a deep breath. "The one I told you to stay away from?"

"Yeah, that one. I'm sorry."

He took a deep breath before he replied. "I'm the one that owes the apology," he said. "I overreacted and I apologize. That case is a minefield and I was hoping to keep you away from it."

"Thanks. I guess."

"I know McGrath was involved in that situation and still is. We need to get something on him so we can send him back where he belongs. Burke's trying to pick up where you left off, but I'm afraid he's in a little over his head. You know how Burke is."

"Yeah. Sort of a loose cannon without any balls."

Hague chuckled at the joke. "He needs your help, if you're willing to get back on the case."

"Let me ask you one thing," Morales said. "Is Kenny Ruffin involved in this somehow?"

"He is now," Hague laughed. "That's what he gets for hanging around with McGrath."

"Okay, what can I do?"

"Burke's out at the old Jackson Oil refinery in Wilmington. You know where that is? Could you meet him out there? Like I said, he needs your help."

Morales had stopped drinking and now she was on her way out to the refinery. The call from Hague surprised her. She knew why he'd taken her off the case — or thought she knew — but why was he inviting her back in? Probably because she'd told him she was still thinking about what he told her to leave alone. For the time being he needed to keep her away from the cover-up or whatever was going on, keep her distracted by the wild goose chase he'd sent Burke out on. The shuttered refinery in Wilmington was the last place you'd look for evidence about a human trafficking and prostitution ring run for pedophiles in downtown L.A. She wondered if Burke was in danger out there, and what risks she'd be taking by going out to help him. No matter. He was her partner and she needed to warn him at least. If he was in on the cover-up she'd better find out about it now. She could handle Burke, she was sure of that.

At Police Headquarters the Commissioner sat on his couch mentoring the same young woman he'd been with earlier that day, the administrative assistant from the third floor, who had again removed her dress. He read aloud from *Being and Nothing-ness,* holding the book in one hand and clasping the other lightly around her throat, imposing a slight restriction of her oxygen supply. This made her groggy, a behavior he did not condone in an administrative assistant. How could a person administer anything or even assist in administering it, let alone follow the text of *Being and Nothingness,* in such a state? In extreme cases this behavior had been known to send him into a self-righteous fury. "Don't fall asleep," he warned her. "We're coming to an exciting part."

"Sorry," she said. "I think you're choking off my air sup-ply."

"You want to survive in this city, you've got to stay alert."

"Right, but— "

"You want to know my number one rule of survival? Stay focused or the media will eat you alive."

The Commissioner was a political animal who'd lived in the zoo for too long, mistaking it for the jungle. The only thing he cared about was survival, which meant: how did he look in the media? *Mayors come and go, voters come and go* (he told his mentees), *but the media are always with us.* When crime statistics were down, when the city had signed a consent decree promis-ing not to shoot drivers at traffic stops, when the jails were crowded enough to provide full employment for the prison guards union, he'd win the media's applause as an enlightened criminologist by advocating low bail, early release, drug coun-seling and community policing. But after a rash of street violence or high-profile crimes, when the public was lathered up about law and order, or when the prison population fell dangerously low, he'd wow the reporters — off the record, of course — with hard-headed realism and refreshing candor. *The best way to deter crime,* he'd tell them, *is to put the criminals in jail before they commit it. It's as simple as that. We can do our job if the courts will only let us do it.* Not everyone agreed with that philosophy of law enforcement. But no matter how the pendulum swung, the Commissioner was lauded as an exemplary public servant with Ivy League credentials who offered advancement to minorities and mentoring to female employees in the department, and grew prize-winning roses in his garden. He read important, difficult books — the kind the reporters had pretended to read in college — and was famous for engaging his staff in serious philosophical discussion.

"I'm sorry if I'm keeping you awake," he snapped at the administrative assistant. "Let me give you the bottom line on modern philosophy. There aren't any moral absolutes. Right and wrong, good and evil — they're just constructs dreamed up by the ruling class (that includes me) to advance its own power. You have to create your own morality through an act of will."

"Really?"

"In other words, you can do whatever you want. Or I should say: *I* can do whatever I want."

"That sounds evil to me."

"No," the Commissioner laughed. "There's no such thing as evil, remember?"

"I'm getting uncomfortable with this," she said, trying to squirm away.

"It doesn't matter if you're uncomfortable," he laughed again. "All I'd have to do is squeeze a little harder and you wouldn't even exist."

The speaker phone on the side table buzzed and the Commissioner reached over and pressed the button to answer. Hague's gravely voice rasped out: "We're taking McGrath out to the refinery. Ruffin got away."

"Remember what I told you, Hague?" the Commissioner said. "No more screw-ups."

"I'm sorry, sir. It won't—"

"You're right it won't happen again," the Commissioner interrupted. "That was your last chance. I'll pick up Burke in the chopper and handle this myself."

He pushed the "off" button on the speaker phone and tossed the woman carelessly onto the floor.

"Get the hell out of here."

The police van sped down the 110 toward Wilmington with the Cadillac following three cars behind. Two vehicles trailed the Cadillac — a red F-150 pickup driven by a man in a black jumpsuit, black boots and black knit cap, and a silver Maserati convertible driven by a blond giant with a killer tan. The van took the exit for the service road to the Jackson Oil refinery and the other vehicles followed.

Derek held his phone to his ear as he drove. "I can't reach him," he heard Shanise say. "His phone's out of service."

"He's not going to kill his father," Derek said. "I won't let that happen."

"Derek, what are you talking about?"

He couldn't bring himself to tell Shanise what he'd witnessed at Bank of America Plaza. His own father died in a car crash when he was fourteen, about the age when he both idolized him and wanted to kill him. Derek had nothing to do with the accident but he'd felt angry and guilty about it all his life. At first those emotions led him to petty crime, then not so petty crime, and he'd landed in juvenile detention after facing the same temptations that Jayden seemed to be succumbing to now. He'd had a lucky break when a stern but sympathetic judge invited him to join the Marines. Basic training toughened him up and gave him the self-confidence he'd been lacking, and in Afghanistan he found an outlet for the "heroics" that so frightened Shanise. He'd never told her the details of what he did in the war — it was brutal but a lot of it wasn't heroic. Now he was afraid to tell her what Jayden had done at the bank plaza. And he was ashamed that he'd frozen before he could do anything to stop him. He'd never tell anybody about that.

"I've got my gun and I'll use it," he told Shanise, "if that's what I have to do to stop him. He's not going to kill his father."

"What are you talking about?"

"Just what I said."

"You're not going to shoot Jayden!"

"No, baby," Derek said. "I'm going to shoot Ruffin."

Morales's phone rang a few minutes later, just as she noticed the sign for the refinery service road. It was Shanise and she was sobbing, almost unable to speak.

"Derek's following Kenny," she said, "and he says he's going to kill him."

"Where are they?"

"Derek's in his truck somewhere, I don't know where. He's talking crazy talk about Jayden killing Kenny and how he's going to kill Kenny before Jayden kills him."

"Why would Jayden kill Kenny?"

"He wouldn't," Shanise said. 'It's just Derek talking crazy, he's having some kind of a lapse. He got pretty messed up in Afghanistan."

"Is he armed?"

"Yeah, he's got his whole arsenal with him."

Morales waited until the crying stopped and said, "Shanise, there's not much we can do until we know where they are. Can you give me the license number to Derek's truck? I'll phone it in and maybe somebody will see him."

Shanise started sobbing again. "I'm afraid somebody's going to get killed."

28

The abandoned Jackson Oil refinery was a jungle of rusting tanks and pipes and sheds and catwalks twisting around a decrepit main building that looked like an ancient airplane hangar, a labyrinth of roads and pathways linking the razor-wired perimeter with oil-blackened sheds and equipment and sludge ponds and parking lots where stunted weeds sprouted from cracks in the asphalt. The place had served a purpose once but now it existed only as a Superfund site polluted so deep into the earth's crust that the bankruptcy receiver had given up trying to sell it. It would probably be the last unoccupied piece of real estate in L.A. when the world ended, which would be sooner there than anywhere else. Perfect then as a haven for dirty cops, a burnt-out inferno where they could celebrate their crimes and avoid any reckoning for them.

A lone security guard waved the police van through the main gate and watched it park on the blistered pavement in front of the hangar-like main building, where the Toyota Land Cruiser had just arrived. Ruffin, following in the Cadillac, cruised past the gate on the service road with his headlights off. He slowed down enough to see Vigil and Harbison pulling McGrath out of the van and frog-marching him to the door. He saw Kimberly swivel out, clutching her handbag as she strutted toward the building. Then the cops yanked Jayden out the tailgate door and Ruffin drove on in an agony of fear and determination.

On the inside, the high-ceilinged hangar was shadowy and deserted, crowded with crates piled on pallets, hanging chains and pulleys, and grotesque shapes hulking under moldy canvas covers. Braces of ladderlike stairways led upwards from both sides of the open main floor to catwalks, platforms, tanks, clusters of piping and enclosed offices used for administrative purposes. On one side the catwalk skirted a large open tank that looked like a swimming pool, only instead of chlorinated water it was filled with oily black sludge that might have come from the La Brea Tar Pits. If you fell off the catwalk into that pool you probably wouldn't be seen again for a million years.

Harbison and Vigil noticed the sludge pool but didn't look down at it as they dragged Jayden up a stairway and along the catwalk to an engineering room located about twenty feet above the main floor. They handcuffed him to a chair, tied a gag across his mouth and locked him in the room.

Darkness had fallen over the unlighted refinery site. Ruffin found a place to park behind a shed along the service road. He had noticed headlights behind him but by the time he parked they had disappeared; evidently the car had turned into the parking lot. He opened the Cadillac's trunk and peered into the pile of junk McGrath had stashed there. Golf clubs, garden tools, a case of iced-tea bottles loaded with gasoline. Fishing gear: two spinning rods, a big tackle box filled with lures and hooks and spools of line, an elaborate canvas fishing vest with dozens of pockets and pouches. And there was the blue United Airlines flight bag Chung had brought to Bank of America Plaza, stuffed with bundles of $100 bills. Twenty or thirty of them — Ruffin didn't take the time to count them. He emptied the tackle box and stuffed the cash into it, covering it with a rag and the lures and spools and other tackle. Then he tossed the empty flight bag into a cluster of sedge growing next to the shed. He put on the fishing vest and loaded eight Molotov cocktails into its pockets along with a box of matches, the rope and the wire cutters. He dumped everything out of the golf bag except the 5-iron and stashed the axe handle and the tire iron inside it like arrows in a quiver. Then he slung the golf bag over his shoulder and headed toward the razor-wire fence. He cut his way through the fence with the wire cutters and squeezed his way into the refinery property. There was an open space filled with gravel between the fence and an elevated bundle of pipes that led to an oil tank beside the main building. He crossed the gravel and edged along the pipes toward the tank, treading as lightly as possible. He was afraid of what might happen if he jiggled the Molotov cocktails.

On the other side of the oil tank a man wearing a black jump suit and a black knit hat crouched with a 9-mm SIG Sauer semi-automatic in his hand, listening as Ruffin crunched across the gravel. He pulled a mask over his face and waited in the shadows.

Olaf the Pool Boy had trailed Ruffin to the refinery site in the Watersons' Maserati convertible, dimming his headlights before Ruffin noticed where he parked. At Bank of America Plaza, it had taken him a few minutes to get back on his feet after Ruffin knocked him down and kicked him in the head. The kick made it personal between him and Ruffin. He wasn't

going to let that prick escape even if Bob Waterson called off
the hit. Luckily he still had his 9-mm Heckler & Koch — and
the silencer — but somehow he'd lost his phone, which left
him unable to call the Watersons to explain what had happened. That was one of those trade-offs that life always seemed
to offer. The Watersons wouldn't be happy to hear that he'd
missed grabbing the money and let both McGrath and Ruffin
escape. If his time as their pool boy had taught him anything, it
was that you don't want to make the Watersons unhappy,
especially Joanne. There were usually some fatalities involved.

What was more important? he asked himself. Finding the
money or whacking Ruffin and McGrath? Probably six of one
and half a dozen of the other. A hundred grand was nothing
to sniff at. But as Bob always said, this was a funny business
they were in. Sometimes killing people was more important
than money. It was the principle of the thing.

Morales stopped along the service road to phone in
Derek's license number with an order that he be stopped and
questioned, with a presumption that he was armed and dangerous. She tried calling Ruffin's phone but got no answer. If
she'd had any idea where Ruffin was, she would have gone
there and left Burke to fend for himself. She knew this trip to
the refinery was just a side show to keep her away from the
money drop Hague had set up with McGrath. Was Burke in on
the ruse? She'd always thought Burke was just lazy and stupid,
but after she talked to Hague she wondered if he was dirty too.
You make allowances for your partner you don't make for
anyone else, not for your boyfriend or your father or even your

mother. She'd looked the other way too many times and now she could see where that had taken her. If Burke was involved with Hague in an elaborate cover-up of the Luisa Salazar shooting that was somehow tied in with the underage prostitution ring of eight years before, she had let herself be lured into a trap. Almost willingly, it would seem. That's the flip side of making allowances for your partner. When he abuses your confidence, crosses you, sells you out, you want to bring him down yourself. You want to be there to make him face up to what he's done. That's what anyone would want in the same situation, Morales thought.

It was the biggest mistake she ever made.

At the refinery, the guard waved her through the gate as if he was expecting her. She saw the black and white LAPD van and the Toyota Land Cruiser. She could see the uniformed cops Harbison and Vigil standing inside the door. She recognized them and they nodded to her as she walked in. She looked around for Burke and didn't see him.

"Where's Detective Burke?" she asked Harbison.

"He'll be here in a few minutes," Harbison said.

Duvaloy and Strausser also looked familiar. She watched in disbelief as they wrestled McGrath onto a folding metal chair and strapped him down with a leather belt. A woman in a miniskirt, halter top and knee-high boots stood over him swishing the strap on her handbag.

"Shoot him if he tries to escape," Kimberly told Strausser.

"I thought you were a whore," McGrath said to Kimberly.

"I'm a cop, you dumb shit."

"I guess I shoulda known," McGrath said. "There's guards at San Quentin give a better blowjob than the one I got from you."

She thrashed him across the face with her handbag strap.

"Am I under arrest?" McGrath yelled. "Cause if I am, I got a right to—"

She whipped him again, this time with the whole purse.

Duvaloy wrapped his big hands around McGrath's throat and shook him like a doll.

"Okay," he said, "here's your Miranda warning. Everything you say—"

"Or even think about saying," Kimberly broke in.

"—can and will be held against you."

Duvaloy punched him hard and he passed out.

Kimberly laughed. "Did you mention that he has the right to remain silent?"

As Ruffin groped his way around the oil tank, a police helicopter suddenly throbbed overhead, scorching the ground with its searchlights. Ruffin dove for cover under the mass of elevated pipes just in time to avoid the searchlight. In the corner of his eye he saw a shadowy figure scurry under another set of pipes — when he whirled around it was gone. He backed up through the darkness and climbed a rusty ladder to an elevated catwalk, a narrow grill that ran toward the hangar about twenty feet off the ground.

From the catwalk he watched the helicopter land in the parking lot, pounding out noise and wind under bright flickering lights. Burke and a heavy bald man in a dark suit climbed down and went inside and the chopper killed its engine. Ruffin remembered the gasoline jars in his vest pockets — he had to be careful. It was too soon even to think about throwing any Molotov cocktails. The hangar looked like it would last about thirty seconds if it caught on fire. And Jayden was in there somewhere. Whoever that shadow was — it must have been a security guard or a cop — he couldn't let him interfere with what he needed to do. He reached into the golf bag and pulled out the axe handle. There was also a golf club he could use if he needed another weapon. With the gas bottles in his pockets he couldn't let himself get drawn into hand to hand combat.

The heavy bald man who got off the helicopter with Burke was the Commissioner. He had a broad friendly face but it might as well have been a mask. He was more a politician than a cop, well liked by those who didn't know him, despised by those who did. That night he must have been in one of his less friendly moods. When he walked into the hangar with Burke, he didn't notice Morales standing beside the door. All he saw was McGrath slumped unconscious on the folding metal chair. "Did he give you any names?" he asked Kimberly.

She pulled a cigarette out of her tiny handbag and shook her head.

Morales stepped out of the shadows and raised her voice. "What's going on here, sir?"

The Commissioner smiled as he recognized her. They had met at a luncheon honoring Hague on his twenty-fifth service anniversary. "Here's what going on, Detective," he said.

"Kenny Ruffin killed our confidential informant Alonzo Payne. Next he's going to kill McGrath."

Morales glanced at McGrath, who opened one eye, just to let her know he was conscious, and shut it as soon as she saw him.

"Is Ruffin here?" Morales asked.

"And then he's going to kill the kid who took a shot at him downtown," the Commissioner went on, ignoring her question.

"That kid is his son, by the way," Burke said.

"I don't believe this," Morales said.

"The guy's an animal," the Commissioner explained. "What can I say? We tried incarceration and that didn't work. When he finishes his killing spree, we're going to find him and take him down in a blaze of gunfire. I wouldn't be surprised if some cops earn commendations for their work. You could be one of them, Detective."

Morales turned to leave, but her way was blocked by Duvaloy and Strausser, who grabbed her gun and locked her arms. There was no point in resisting. If she shook them off she'd have to go through Harbison and Vigil, who blocked the door with their Berettas drawn.

"So the question for you, Detective," the Commissioner smiled — "and this is what the philosophers call an either/or — is are you a cop or not?"

"You make me sick."

"That's sort of a cliché, isn't it? Something you saw in an old movie?"

"You may be the biggest piece of shit in the jungle," Morales said, "but you're still a piece of shit."

The Commissioner shrugged and rolled his eyes toward Burke. "Hell is other people," he said. "You see it every day."

"It's like I told you," Burke said. "She's got attitude problems."

"You realize the hoops I have to jump through when we lose a female officer?" he asked Burke.

"She knows too much," Burke said. "Way too much."

"Okay," the Commissioner shrugged. "Shit happens." He turned to Duvaloy. "Take her upstairs. We'll let Ruffin do the honors when we catch him."

Duvaloy and Strausser dragged Morales upstairs to an executive office on the opposite side of the hangar from the engineering room where Jayden was held. They punched her in the kidneys a couple times to keep her quiet, tied her to a metal chair and locked her in the room.

As the two men came back down, the Commissioner pulled McGrath's head up by the hair to get a better look at his face. McGrath, still playing possum, kept his eyes closed and his neck limp.

"I almost forgot what an asshole looks like," the Commissioner said.

"He's been in San Quentin for eight years," Strausser said.

"Takes its toll on a guy," Duvaloy added.

Strausser pinched McGrath's upper lip and pulled it back for a look at his prison teeth. "He's got a much nicer smile than he used to have."

"Damn waste of the taxpayers' money," Duvaloy grumbled.

"He'll need those teeth a little while longer," the Commissioner said, "along with his tongue." He let go of McGrath's hair and his head slumped. "You know he loves to talk."

As Ruffin crept along the elevated catwalk, twenty feet over a deadly thicket of pipes and rusty equipment, a man in a black jumpsuit, a black mask and a black knit hat sprang out of the darkness and attacked him with leather-gloved hands. He came at Ruffin like a giant action figure, more terrifying in appearance than in anything he actually did. Ruffin spun around to avoid his grasp but dropped the axe handle as he struggled to keep his balance on the narrow catwalk. The axe handle bounced on the catwalk but didn't fall over the edge.

With eight Molotov cocktails in his vest pockets, Ruffin couldn't fight the way he'd learned to fight, attacking with both fists, absorbing his opponent's punches to head and body until he powered his way through them. Instead he fought defensively, skittering backwards, kicking, flailing his fists, trying to keep his assailant from taking him down. The man leaped forward and Ruffin dodged again, deflecting the blows. After absorbing a swipe to the side of his head, Ruffin whirled back with a roundhouse punch that knocked the man down and almost over the edge. He clung to the rim of the catwalk with one gloved hand.

Ruffin thought about stomping it and kicking him the rest of the way down into the rusty scrap heap that probably would have killed him. But that wasn't what he was there for. He was there to save Jayden, not to kill somebody he didn't need to kill. Instead he bent over and pulled the man up.

That act of mercy was a mistake. As soon as he was on his feet, the man pulled out a 9-mm SIG Sauer and pointed it at Ruffin's head. "Get the hell out of here before I kill you," he said in a hoarse whisper.

Who was this mystery man? He couldn't have been a cop in that get-up. Why didn't he just pull the trigger? And why was he whispering?

"You ain't gonna shoot me, Batman," Ruffin said, taking a chance. He bent down and scooped up the axe handle and as he straightened back up he lashed out and slammed the man on the side of the head. The man dropped the SIG Sauer and crumbled unconscious on the catwalk.

"You don't want them to know you're here any more than I do," Ruffin said. "Whoever you are."

Ruffin pulled off the goggles, then the hat and the mask, and recognized the man whose picture Shanise had shown him on her phone.

"Shit."

He left Derek where he was and padded down the catwalk toward the hangar. Only after he'd gone inside did it occur to him that he'd left Derek's gun where it fell.

Big Olaf watched from the shadows as Ruffin and Derek fought it out. He had no idea who Derek was, even after Ruffin pulled off his mask and goggles, and he didn't want to risk shooting the wrong guy. Derek might have been a cop, possibly one of the dirty cops on Bob Waterson's payroll. He left Derek where he fell and followed Ruffin down the catwalk, stopping only to retrieve Derek's SIG Sauer. That was a brand often used by hitmen—he'd never used one before and was eager to try it out.

Strausser and Duvaloy dragged McGrath up a metal staircase to a bleak industrial room on the upper level. The room had a high window on one end and an oil storage tank at the other end. Near the window a rope hung from a pulley controlled by an electronic switch on the wall. They hog-tied McGrath's wrists and ankles and lashed them behind him with the rope, which they hoisted toward the ceiling using the electronic switch. The pain made him cry out. He had to stop pretending to be unconscious.

Burke and the Commissioner stood in front of him, smiling. "Cat, you and I go way back," the Commissioner said, "so I want to keep this friendly. Have you ever heard of Jean-Paul Sartre?"

"Used to play for the Rangers, didn't he?" McGrath asked.

"No, he was a writer," the Commissioner said. "He wrote a book called *Nausea,* which sums up the way I feel when I look at you. And he wrote a play called *No Exit.* That must be how you feel right now."

"Come to think of it, the guy I'm thinking of played for the Bruins," McGrath said.

"I need some information."

"You'll get your information when I get my money."

"You got your money this afternoon."

"I never got it. That whore—"

"It was brought to within fifty feet of you," the Commissioner said.

"I still never got it."

"Let's cut the crap," the Commissioner said. "No more fun and games. What I need are the names of everybody you've ever talked to about our little escapade of eight years ago."

"You mean when you strangled that innocent little Chinese girl?"

The Commissioner punched him hard in the face. "She wasn't an innocent little girl," he said. "She was a whore, and you brought her to me yourself."

"Not to strangle, I didn't."

"She laughed at me," the Commissioner said bitterly. "That was a big mistake."

"No, I think she nailed that one right on the head."

"But it doesn't matter now. As you'll soon find out, whether someone's alive or dead only matters as long as they're alive."

"No shit."

"Your death is not an event in your life. Nietzsche said that."

"You're nuts."

The Commissioner swung McGrath into the concrete wall and watched him bounce back.

"Just let me ask you one thing," McGrath said, stalling for time. "This whole thing with the underage Chinese girls — that was something you set up with Chung's uncle, right?"

"It was a Waterson racket from day one. Chung's uncle just provided the venue. I got the pick of the litter for making sure the department looked the other way."

He reared back to punch McGrath again as he swung by.

"I'm willing to let bygones be bygones," McGrath said. "Just give me the money you promised me for saying you was a Russian."

"Who have you talked to about this?"

"Nobody. Not a living soul."

The Commissioner gave him another shove into the wall and raised his fist to strike again.

"Other than the Warden up at San Quentin," McGrath said. "I think I mentioned it while he was blowing me."

This time the Commissioner nodded at Burke, who hammered McGrath as hard as he could. Blood spouted from McGrath's mouth and nose. One of his eyes was swelling shut.

"Did you tell any of the other prisoners?" the Commissioner asked.

"I never talked to those scumbags if I could help it."

The Commissioner reached in his pocket and pulled out a pair of pruning shears. "I use these at home for pruning my roses," he said, clicking them in front of McGrath's face. "You've got to be careful you don't catch your fingers in them. Or any other body appendages."

"Come to think of it," McGrath said, "there was one prisoner I told about it. Name of Grijalva. Used to have the bunk next to mine."

The Commissioner nodded to Burke. "Call up to San Quentin and tell them to take care of this Grijalva." He rattled his pruning shears next to McGrath's ear and smiled.

Burke looped a gag across McGrath's mouth and shoved a hood over his head, and they headed for the door. "You can hang around here as long as you like," the Commissioner said over his shoulder. "I'll come back to finish my pruning later."

Ruffin crept along the catwalk toward the hangar, where he could see light in an upstairs window. As he came closer, he heard McGrath's voice wailing bitterly from inside the window. The voice was frantic, muffled by the gag, distorted so much that Ruffin couldn't understand what he was saying. Peering down through the window, he saw McGrath dangling beneath him — shirtless, hooded, gagged, hog-tied and howling with pain and indignation.

He cracked the window, silently broke and removed the glass, looped his rope around a pipe behind him and hoisted himself down, dropping the golf bag on the floor.

The hooded McGrath thought his tormenters had returned. "Now what are you gonna do?" he gurgled. "Cut my balls off with your pruning shears? I'll talk, for Christ's sake! Just let me down!"

Ruffin pulled off the hood and the gag, but left McGrath dangling.

"Ruffin!" McGrath said. "Thank God it's you. Cut me down!"

Instead Ruffin gave McGrath a shove, swinging him from side to side.

"You got here in the nick of time," McGrath said, trying to catch his breath. "Them sons of bitches come back in here, I'm gonna kick the shit out of them."

"I just had a little chat with Alonzo Payne," Ruffin said calmly. "He told me it's you he been shooting at all along."

"I suspected that," McGrath admitted. "Now will you cut me the hell down?"

"I thought you was my friend," Ruffin said.

"I'm the best friend you ever had," McGrath said. "Cut me down and I'll share that money with you."

"You never got the money."

"Yeah, but I know where it is."

Ruffin knew McGrath was lying, which pissed him off even more. He gave him a vicious shove and swung him into the wall. "You put me out there to take a bullet that had your name on it."

"I never said it was you they was trying to kill," McGrath said, wincing as he hit the wall. "I never told you that."

"Nobody does that to me."

"I'm dying up here, Ruffin. Cut me down!"

Olaf looked down on Ruffin and McGrath through the high window Ruffin had broken to get inside, threading the silencer on his 9-mm Heckler & Koch. From up there he had a clear shot at both of them, and McGrath's gyrations brought in an element of challenge and skill that was often lacking in his work. For somebody who grew up hunting wolverines in northern Minnesota, being a hit man had turned out to be a pretty boring job, though a lot better than being a pool boy. On a day he might have spent hosing down the patio furniture or skimming leaves off the pool — or worse, hiding in his cabana from the brats — a moment like this was to be savored. Why hurry it along? If he listened he might find out where the money was.

Grinning like a bear, Ruffin reached in the golf bag and pulled out the axe handle. "You got this all wrong, McGrath," he said. "I ain't here to rescue you. I'm here to whup your brains out with this axe handle."

"Shit, Ruffin," McGrath said, "you didn't need to drive all the way out here to do that. What do you think them sons of bitches brought me here for? They're gonna kill me. Then they're gonna pin it on you."

"What're you talking about?" Ruffin asked.

"I heard 'em making plans," McGrath said. "They said you're gonna kill me, just like you killed Alonzo."

"I didn't kill Alonzo."

"They did, then," McGrath said. "And made it look like it was you."

"No shit."

"And then — I don't know if you're gonna like this — you're gonna kill a cop."

"What cop?"

"Morales."

"Shit."

"It gets worse," McGrath said. He looked desperate, his eyes rolling almost out of his head.

"How could it get worse than killing a cop?" Ruffin asked.

"Let me down and I'll tell you."

"Tell me first, then maybe I'll think about letting you down."

"After you kill Morales," McGrath said, almost in a whisper, "they say you're gonna kill Jayden."

In a fury Ruffin hurled McGrath into the concrete wall. "The hell I am!"

McGrath cried out and tried to twist away, swinging crazily. Olaf tried to keep his aim fixed on McGrath but it was hard with the rope blocking his view and all McGrath's twisting and flailing around.

"Don't you get it, Ruffin?" McGrath cried out. "I'm on your side!"

Ruffin hesitated. "I let you down," he said, "you gonna help me rescue Jayden?"

"I swear I will," McGrath swore. "I absolutely will."

"And then Morales?"

McGrath balked at that. "Rescue a cop?" Sweat poured off his forehead. "I don't know about that. I got my principles."

Ruffin picked up the golf bag and headed toward the door.

Olaf turned the Heckler & Koch toward Ruffin, figuring this was his last chance to whack him before he left the room. McGrath knew where the money was, so who needed Ruffin?

"Wait a minute!" McGrath pleaded, and Ruffin turned back around.

Just then the door rattled and Ruffin had just enough time to jump behind the oil storage tank before it opened. In walked Harbison — he'd been sent to check on McGrath. "Hey, you asshole," he said to McGrath. "How'd you get that hood off?"

Olaf recognized Harbison as one of the cops from the bank plaza, probably one of Waterson's dirty cops. He was tempted to call out and warn him as Ruffin glided up behind him and hammered him with the axe handle.

Harbison wobbled and went down on his knees. "All the way down!" Ruffin said, hammering him again until he slumped to the floor. "I ain't gonna axe you again!"

McGrath howled with glee.

"Quiet now," Ruffin said. "They'll all be coming in." He lowered McGrath with the electronic switch and cut him loose. The two of them stripped off Harbison's shirt, slipped the gag and hood over his face and hoisted him up, dangling and moaning, where McGrath had been.

And it wasn't a minute too soon. The door rattled again and this time both Ruffin and McGrath hid behind the storage tank. They heard the Commissioner snapping his pruning shears as he walked toward the hanging man. McGrath slipped the 5-iron out of the golf bag and waited.

Olaf recognized the Commissioner from the TV news. What the hell was going on in this place?

The Commissioner punched Harbison hard in the face through the hood. "This is what they call an existential moment, Cat," he said. "Fear and trembling."

He punched him again, knocking him into the wall. "No exit."

Whistling a tune, the Commissioner rattled the pruning shears like castanets in Harbison's ear. "You got ten fingers, I want ten names. You know how to count?"

Harbison grunted wildly, desperately, twisting on the rope like a fish fighting for its life.

"What was that, McGrath?" the Commissioner taunted. "I couldn't quite make out what you said."

Harbison gave up trying to argue and let out a long, unintelligible scream.

"That's more like it," the Commissioner said. "You ready to talk?" But instead of pulling off the hood he punched Harbison again and again, for no reason but the sheer enjoyment of it. McGrath tightened his grip on the 5-iron — those blows were meant for him.

Harbison finally passed out. The Commissioner pulled off the hood and found, instead of McGrath, a bloody semblance of Harbison's face. Before he could react, Ruffin and McGrath leaped at him from behind the tank. Ruffin grappled with him, trying to keep his hand off his gun, while McGrath whaled on his head with the 5-iron. It wasn't long before the Commissioner looked like a heap of dirty laundry on the floor.

Ruffin picked up the gun — it was a .38 caliber Smith & Wesson — and sprang for the door. "We got to find Jayden."

They ran down the stairs to the deserted main floor of the hangar. Voices jangled in one of the upstairs rooms on the other side.

"That's where they took Jayden," McGrath said.

Ruffin stashed the fishing vest packed with Molotov cocktails behind the metal stairway and they crept up to the catwalk that led to the engineering room. Ruffin turned off the safety and held the Commissioner's .38 in front of him with both hands as they padded along the catwalk. The door stood open and they could see into the room. Jayden, handcuffed to his chair, fought back tears as Burke, Strausser and Kimberly debated what to do with him.

Kimberly inhaled on a cigarette. "I don't see why we need to kill the kid," she said.

"It's the cleanest way to go," Strausser said.

"A couple hours ago he was shooting at his own dad," Burke pointed out. "What kind of kid does that? We're doing the world a favor getting this animal off the streets."

Ruffin felt the blunt steel of a gun barrel jammed into his back. On his right he could see Vigil holding a Beretta against McGrath's neck. It was Duvaloy behind him, pushing him into the room. "I'll take that," Duvaloy said, reaching for the Commissioner's gun in Ruffin's hand.

Burke laughed when they entered the room. "Ruffin! You're just in time to shoot your son."

"Jayden!" Ruffin yelled. He spun around, grabbed Duvaloy's arm and wrestled for the Commissioner's gun. It went off with a deafening blast and landed on the floor. Burke leaped up and Ruffin stopped him with a punch to the jaw. He tottered and fell backwards but Duvaloy was on Ruffin's back, pistol whipping him from behind with his Beretta until he went down. Vigil had McGrath pinned on the floor. It all happened in the space of two or three seconds. The bullet had blasted a hole in the wall about a foot from Jayden's head. Jayden burst into tears.

Strausser and Duvaloy handcuffed Ruffin and McGrath to a pair of folding chairs and pistol whipped them until blood dripped on the floor. Ruffin spit at Burke and Burke punched him hard enough to knock out a tooth, which he spit at Strausser

Burke pulled out a fresh Beretta and handed it to Strausser, wiping it clean with his handkerchief. "Whack Ruffin first so you can make sure his prints are on this when he shoots the kid," he told Strausser. Then he smiled at Ruffin. "That last little touch is for Shanise. Something to remember you by."

"What about McGrath?" Strausser asked.

"You know the script," Burke said. "Ruffin kills him too, just like he killed Alonzo."

He turned to leave with Duvaloy, Vigil and Kimberly, who looked like she might be sick. "Come on," Burke told them. "We need to take care of Morales."

29

After Burke and the others left, Strausser stood in front of Ruffin hefting the gun Burke had handed him. He had his orders: Shoot Ruffin first, then wipe the gun clean and put it in Ruffin's hand to shoot Jayden and McGrath. Better not get any blood on the prints or the medical examiner might be suspicious. He'd heard of such things happening.

"You right or left handed?" he asked Ruffin.

"You expect me to answer that?"

"We want it to look as realistic as possible when you kill your son," Strausser grinned.

"I'm right handed," Ruffin said.

"That means you're left handed," Strausser smirked. "You think I'm stupid?"

The answer was yes, but Ruffin didn't say it. He was right handed. He rocked in his chair, trying to tip it over. "I ain't killing my son!"

Jayden sobbed violently. "You killed Alonzo."

"I didn't kill Alonzo," Ruffin shouted. "Burke killed Alonzo." He pleaded with Jayden to believe this one thing about him in the last seconds of his life. "That cop that just walked out of here, Burke, he killed Alonzo. He cut Alonzo's throat with a knife. I saw him do it."

Morales had struggled to the point of exhaustion to free herself from the ropes Strausser and Duvaloy had lashed around her. It was hopeless. She couldn't separate herself from the metal chair. They meant to kill her — knowing that made her nauseous and faint, hyperventilating, her heart racing as if in an attempt to escape — and Ruffin would be forced to do it, which made her even sicker. She prayed, though she felt a little ashamed, it was so self-serving — too little, too late — and she felt more angry and desperate than contrite. Nobody seemed to be listening anyway. She only hoped she'd be able to forgive Ruffin before she died.

Derek had regained consciousness where Ruffin left him on the outside catwalk. His head throbbed from the blow with the axe handle but he had no trouble standing up. He'd landed on his gun when he fell. He picked it up and climbed down into the pitch darkness that surrounded the hangar. He had no idea how much time had passed since Ruffin knocked him out.

He circled the hangar to a back entrance where the door had been left open. Lights were on inside and he could hear voices jangling in the distance. He found a shadowy lookout point behind a pallet piled with crates and rusty equipment. From there he watched Ruffin and McGrath come down a metal staircase and cross the open floor, then pad their way up another stairs on the other side, where light gleamed from an open door. He saw Duvaloy and Vigil sneak up behind them with guns drawn and shove them into the light. He heard Ruffin shout Jayden's name, and he heard the gunshot and the struggle that followed it. Then the crashing and shouting stopped and he lost sight of what went on in that room. The only thing he could hear was somebody crying. He couldn't be sure if it was Jayden but his clenching gut told him that it was. His hands were shaking.

He heard voices — men's voices and a woman's voice too — and after a minute he saw Burke come downstairs with two men and a woman in a mini-skirt. One of the men was a uniformed cop, Hispanic-looking and vaguely familiar. The other was one of the men who'd grabbed Jayden at the bank plaza. His partner, the big hulking blond guy who looked like Arnold Schwartzenegger, was still in that room. And Ruffin was still in there, with Jayden. They must have left them together so Jayden could kill him — or maybe it was the other way around. Either way, he wasn't going to let it happen.

He heard more shouting, more sobbing, which could only be coming from Jayden. He had no time to waste. He turned off the safety on his SIG Sauer and pulled down his mask. Then he darted across the open floor and up the stairs to the catwalk, his hands trembling. He sprinted down to the open door, the door to the engineering room, and the first thing he saw was Ruffin sitting on a chair. He fired three shots.

Ruffin had heard him coming, then saw him coming. In the last instant before the shooting started he toppled his chair forward with a violent heave and knocked Strausser into the path of the bullets. He kept rolling, chair and all, smashing into Derek's shins and knocking him down. Derek was trapped beneath him, unable to use his gun. Struggling, furious — in a second or two he would wrench himself free.

"The guy you just shot is a cop," Ruffin said.

"I was aiming at you," Derek said.

"He was about to kill Jayden."

"I'm still gonna kill you."

"Derek!" Jayden shouted. "He's trying to save me."

Ruffin rolled off and let Derek stand up. Strausser was unconscious, bleeding from a chest wound. Derek found the key to the handcuffs in his pocket and used it to unlock Jayden. Jayden threw his arms around Derek and wouldn't let go.

"That's my dad," Jayden said. "He's trying to save me."

Derek let Jayden keep hanging on while he unlocked Ruffin, then McGrath. Ruffin stuck Strausser's Beretta in his pocket and picked up the Commissioner's .38 off the floor.

McGrath didn't move but his eyes were wide open. He was soaked with sweat and blood and maybe a couple of other body fluids. "I think I'll stay right here," he said.

Ruffin poked the Commissioner's gun into his ribs and smiled. "You're coming with me, partner."

When he heard the three gunshots, Burke assumed that his orders had been carried out: Ruffin, Jayden, McGrath — in that order.

"Three down, one to go," he said. He glanced at Duvaloy and they hurried up a stairway toward the executive office where Morales had been handcuffed to a chair.

Vigil excused himself to use the bathroom. As soon as Burke and Duvaloy were out of earshot, he slipped around a corner with his phone. He called a number where he didn't need to identify himself. "Things are getting out of control," he said into the phone. "Better get the team over here fast."

In the executive office, Duvaloy ungagged Morales as Burke aimed his Beretta at her head. "Say your prayers," Burke said.

Morales's moment of piety passed at the sight of Burke holding a gun to her head. "Burn in hell," she said. "That's my prayer for you."

"Don't you have one for yourself?"

"If I only have one prayer, why waste it on myself if I can use it to send you to hell?"

"It's too bad about you, Morales," Burke said. "You could have made a good cop."

Ruffin retrieved the fishing vest from under the stairs and slipped out the Molotov cocktails and the box of matches. He lined up the bottles on the floor next to the stairs.

"You're gonna need fuses," McGrath said.

"What?"

"What planet did you grow up on, Ruffin?" McGrath said. "Every Boy Scout knows a Molotov cocktail needs a fuse." He tore some strips off his T-shirt, soaked them with gas and stuffed them into the necks of the iced-tea bottles. Then he pointed up the stairs to the office where Burke and Duvaloy had gone to kill Morales. "See that door up there?" he said. "That's where they got Morales. You want to save her, now's your chance. Hand me them matches and I'll start serving the iced tea whenever you're ready."

"Okay, wait." Ruffin pointed to a stairway at the other end of the catwalk. "I'll go up over there and circle back around.

Wait till I'm up there so I can start shooting when they run out of the room."

He hurried to the stairway and climbed up, signaling when he was near the top. McGrath waved back at him with a crazed smile. Contrary to what he'd expected that morning, he wasn't having a good day. He'd been swindled out of his money, betrayed by a whore who turned out to be a cop, beaten to a pulp and strung up like a hog in a slaughterhouse. Now he was ready to have some fun with the Molotov cocktails. He felt like a kid who'd been put in charge of the fireworks on the Fourth of July.

As Ruffin stalked down the catwalk, winding around the edge of the sludge pool, McGrath lighted two of the cocktails and launched his attack. The bombs exploded in front of the executive office, blowing gas and flames in all directions.

The office door flew open and Duvaloy ran out choking on the smoke. Ruffin was ready for him. He smashed him over the head with the Commissioner's gun, stunning him but not knocking him out. He held him up, staggering, and used him as a shield when Burke charged out, shooting wildly into the flames. Duvaloy took the bullets and went down as Ruffin opened fire and Burke ducked back into the office.

The whole area under the roof had filled with acrid black smoke. The sounds of choking and coughing rattled over the roar of the flames. Morales was tied up somewhere in that office, Ruffin knew. She could suffocate if he didn't pull her out of there.

Burke was trapped too — he couldn't stay in the office longer than another thirty seconds. He burst out, firing rapidly, and Ruffin had to back onto a small platform adjoining the catwalk that stuck out over the sludge pool. Looking down, he realized that jumping down wasn't an option. He was trapped on that platform — he couldn't go any farther without landing in the sludge and he couldn't go back the way he came. His only hope was to kill Burke before Burke killed him. For an instant the smoke billowed away and he had a clear shot. He pulled the trigger but the Smith & Wesson just clicked. It was out of ammunition.

Burke stalked forward, eager to make the kill. He smiled at Ruffin with that sadistic smile of his, knowing that one way or another Ruffin was finished. It would only take one shot. He wanted to see Ruffin topple into the sludge tank and disappear.

At that moment McGrath launched his second attack, mounting halfway up the stairs with two more cocktails. He lobbed them up and they exploded next to Burke before Burke could take that last shot at Ruffin. He panicked and retreated into the office and slammed the door behind him.

Ruffin reached in his pocket and found Strausser's Beretta. He'd almost forgotten about Strausser's Beretta. There was still hope for Morales if he could get into that office. He ran back on the catwalk and toward the office through the flames, shooting at the lock on the door. Burke fired back like a one-man army from the other side.

Somehow in that gun battle — it was probably one of Ruffin's bullets that did it — Morales was shot. The chair she was tied to toppled over and she lay on the floor expecting to die.

From the top of the stairs McGrath lobbed two more bombs, which exploded in front of the door. Ruffin had to stand back, overcome by the heat and smoke. The flames had spread across the roof beams to the other side of the hangar.

Burke burst out shooting and ran down the catwalk in the opposite direction.

Downstairs, the Commissioner stumbled through the shadows and the burning debris behind the tanks and pallets toward the back door. He'd regained consciousness on the cement floor of the room where he'd tortured McGrath. His head was bleeding — it felt like somebody had pummeled it with the 5-iron that lay on the floor beside him. He couldn't remember where he was but he knew he'd better get out of there. Harbison hung over him, bloody and moaning like the crucified Christ in an early Netherlandish painting (that was another of the Commissioner's interests, early Netherlandish painting), but without the halo.

Vigil watched the Commissioner from a distance and followed him outside.

Morales, lying wounded on the floor and choking on the smoke, dragged herself out to the catwalk. She found Duvaloy — unconscious but still alive — and dug the key to the handcuffs out of his pocket. Unlocking the cuffs, she groped through the warm blood oozing out of him for his gun. When she found it she crawled down the catwalk after Ruffin, who'd caught up with Burke about fifty feet away. The flames pushed her back and the smoke blinded and choked her. She heard gun shots and the crack and hiss of exploding pipes as flaming gas jets blocked her path.

Burke had evaded Ruffin's shots and climbed a ladder above the catwalk, hidden by the fire. He perched on it waiting as Ruffin groped through the smoke and flames. As Ruffin passed below, he pounced on Ruffin and clubbed him with his Beretta.

Morales heard angry, desperate voices as the men thrashed around pounding and kicking each other in the final moments of their struggle.

The fire had spread along the oily roof beams to the opposite side of the hangar. A burning beam crashed down on the catwalk in front of the engineering room, where Derek had stayed with Jayden, blocking the door with a wall of flames. Deadly smoke darkened the room. Derek called out for help over the roar of the fire. They were trapped.

On the floor below, McGrath's avid eyes darted from one side of the hangar to the other. The whole upper part was in flames and blanketed with smoke. On his right he heard Ruffin and Burke trying to beat each other's brains out, on his left the shrieks of Derek and Jayden crying out for someone to rescue them. What should he do? He had a chance to run away, but something held him back.

McGrath was no hero. He attributed this not to innate cowardice but to a conscious survival strategy he'd adopted many years before. Except for women (when he had a reasonable chance of getting laid), he never went out of his way to help anyone. That policy had served him well in drug busts, prison riots, and other common situations. But something about this was different. Possibly owing to the lack of oxygen in the air, or because of the fun and excitement he'd had hurling Molotov cocktails at the cops, he felt lightheaded, full of himself, almost invulnerable. And on top of that he detected an odd sensation of righteousness, of wanting to be on the right side. Lives were in danger and he felt himself rising to the occasion. Could he afford to make an exception and be a hero for once in his life?

He heard Derek and Jayden cry out again and started up the stairs, but before he'd gone half way he glimpsed a familiar figure clambering up behind him in a mini-skirt and leather boots, and before he could turn around he felt the unmistakable sensation of a gun barrel digging into his crotch.

"It's me, lover boy," Kimberly said.

He twisted around but she jammed the gun in harder and warned him not to move.

"I think our relationship might have got off to a bad start," he said. "You posing as a hooker and all."

"It would've been better if you knew I was a cop?"

"Sure, I mean—"

"Back slowly down the steps. Nice and easy."

"Don't you think we could still make it work?" McGrath said. "Spend more quality time together, maybe go to counseling—"

"Shut up."

McGrath lost his balance and fell backwards, carrying both of them down the narrow stairs. Kimberly's gun went off but luckily missed hitting either of them. At the bottom he punched her hard in the jaw and twisted her arms behind her with her face jammed against the cement floor. Then he lashed her wrists to the hand rail with the strap from her handbag.

"You son of a bitch!" she screamed.

"Give it some thought," he said. "We still might be able to make a go of it."

"Let me go, you asshole!"

He wadded up what was left of his T-shirt and shoved it in her mouth.

Burke knew about Ruffin's shoulder wound. When he was done pistol-whipping him, he pounded the wounded shoulder over and over again until Ruffin almost passed out, hanging over the edge of the catwalk. He held the Beretta against Ruffin's head and stood up, stepping back to aim a shot that wouldn't look like premeditated murder. Better yet, why not nudge him over the edge and let him break his neck on the concrete floor below?

Behind him, Morales pulled herself forward on her elbows, trying to ignore the searing pain from her wound. She was bleeding out and she didn't know how long she would last. She came to a stop and raised Duvaloy's Beretta in front of her with both hands.

"This wouldn't be happening if you'd killed McGrath like we thought you would," she heard Burke telling Ruffin. "Why do you think we stuck you on that bus?"

Morales fired the gun at Burke, aiming at the middle of his back. The bullet hit him in the left shoulder. He whirled around, firing wildly as Ruffin rolled away. One of his bullets hit Morales.

Ruffin pulled himself up and tried to wrest the gun out of Burke's hand. Burke beat him back but he couldn't use his left arm. Still he wrenched the gun free and whirled back around to shoot Ruffin. Morales fired again.

This time she hit her target and Burke went down. Her head dropped and she let go of the gun. The last thing she heard before she lost consciousness was Ruffin beside her:

"Stay with me, hear?"

He picked her up and carried her down the stairs.

On the parking lot outside, an ambulance arrived and a police helicopter circled for landing. Three squad cars raced in behind the ambulance with their lights flashing and their sirens howling. McGrath tottered in the doorway catching his breath after escaping from Kimberly. From where he stood it appeared that reinforcements had been called in, possibly the entire LAPD if not the U.S. Cavalry.

Thinking quickly — or probably not thinking at all — McGrath lighted and tossed a Molotov cocktail in front of the squad cars, which, when it exploded, collided and crashed to a screeching halt. Half a dozen cops leaped out and ran toward him, shouting and brandishing their guns as he struck a match and lit the fuse of his last cocktail.

"Drop your weapon!" they shouted.

As much as McGrath would have liked to obey, he couldn't simply drop the Molotov cocktail or it would have blown him up along with the cops who gave the order. By then the helicopter had landed and three more cops had jumped out along with the pilot, led by Captain Robert M. Kearney of

LAPD internal affairs, who'd been investigating the Commissioner and his coterie of dirty cops for over two years. So McGrath did the only thing a man in his position could do. He lobbed his last bomb into the cockpit and blew up the helicopter.

As the chopper exploded, Ruffin staggered out of the building carrying Morales, and handed her over to the EMTs from the ambulance. Two cops tried to grab him, but he fought them off and ran back through the smoke and flames to get Jayden and Derek.

"Let him go," Captain Kearney said. "We need to concentrate on getting the rest of the cops out of there."

A half dozen men had tackled McGrath, kicking and punching him as they dragged him away. "Hang on, amigos!" he said. "I just left a woman tied up in there with a T-shirt stuffed in her mouth. I thought she was a whore, but she swears she's a cop."

Back in the hangar, Ruffin climbed the stairs and crawled through the flames and smoke to the room where Jayden and Derek called out for help. He kicked aside the beam that blocked the door and pulled them out of the room, dragging them by the arms as he struggled back down the stairs.

He knew he'd be arrested as soon as the cops figured out who he was. Before they went outside, he reached in his pocket for the keys to the Cadillac. "Derek, listen to me," he said. "You know that old green Cadillac I been driving? You followed it here. You know where I parked, right?"

"Yeah," Derek gasped, barely able to talk,

"I need you to do something. As soon as you can breathe, go over there and look in the trunk. There's a bunch of fishing gear in there. I want Jayden to have it."

"Fishing gear?" Derek said. He was choking and coughing and wobbling on his feet. "Are you nuts?"

"Never mind if I'm nuts," Ruffin said. "I just saved your life, even though you took my woman and you tried to take my son. So you do this for me with no arguments, hear? Get that fishing gear — there's a big brown tackle box in there — get that tackle box out and make sure everything in it goes to Shanise. It's for Jayden."

He pulled out the car keys and stuck them in Derek's hand

Olaf the Pool Boy had missed his chance to kill Ruffin and McGrath when they beat up the Commissioner and then, following them into the hangar, had spent the last half hour hiding behind piles of crates and canvas-shrouded equipment as he watched the bewildering procession of hostages and cops, gun battles and firebombs, hoping somebody or something would tip him off to what had become of the money so he could blow the whole lot of them to kingdom come. Now time was running out. The building would collapse in flames in a few minutes. But suddenly he'd gotten lucky. There was Ruffin — bloody, staggering, beaten to shreds — giving this other black guy instructions on where to find the money, even handing him the keys to his car, the green Cadillac he'd parked along the service road. It didn't get any better than this.

Olaf sprang out from his hiding place and grabbed the keys from Derek's hand almost as soon as Ruffin put them there.

Without looking back he jumped away and ran up the stairs Ruffin had staggered down a few minutes before. Ruffin had been fighting with the cops up there, shooting at them, getting shot at — there was no way he'd go up there again. But he did, the crazy man. He scrambled up the stairs with what seemed his last breath and chased Olaf down the catwalk, cornering him on the platform above the sludge pool.

Olaf pulled out the SIG Sauer he'd picked up outside and aimed it at Ruffin, who stopped about six feet in front of him. For Olaf it was a great chance to try out a new weapon. He'd used his Heckler & Koch so many times it wasn't even fun anymore. "It's all over, buddy," he told Ruffin, laughing. He dangled the car keys over the open tank. "If you want your friend to have these keys, why not come and get them?"

Ruffin sprang forward with a roar. Olaf pulled the trigger and nothing happened. Not being familiar with the SIG Sauer, he'd left the safety on by mistake.

Before he could react, Ruffin punched him hard in the face, then grabbed his hair and threw him over the railing into the sludge pool, car keys and all. He landed with an oily splash and sank to the bottom along with the keys. The Pool Boy, it turned out, didn't know how to swim.

Ruffin shook his head in disbelief. "You think Derek don't know how to use a crowbar?" he asked the bubbles gurgling up from the bottom of the tank.

A rescue team brought out Burke, Duvaloy, Strausser and Harbison, miraculously all still alive though badly wounded. When the last team came out with Kimberly, they were met by

Captain Kearney — "Take her downtown," he said — and when Vigil dragged the cowering Commissioner out from behind the hangar, Captain Kearney personally snapped the handcuffs on his bloated wrists. "Good work, Vigil," he said, and then he turned to the Commissioner: "I've been looking forward to this for a long time."

More ambulances and fire trucks arrived as flames engulfed the hangar. Ruffin walked over to McGrath, who'd been handcuffed to the door of a squad car. McGrath's face was bloody, bruised and swollen to about twice its usual size, but Ruffin detected a gleam of satisfaction in his eyes.

"Well, I didn't get my money," McGrath said. "But we sure taught them sons of bitches a thing or two, didn't we?"

For a long minute — before Ruffin himself was snapped in cuffs and shoved into a different car — they stood together looking out over the carnage. They saw:

Four dirty cops on their way to the Emergency Room.

Two more cops — including the Commissioner — being dragged away in handcuffs.

Three wrecked police cars.

A smoldering helicopter.

A refinery collapsing in flames.

"Well, what do you think?" Ruffin asked McGrath. "You think this might be a parole violation?"

30

Ruffin and McGrath spent two nights in the division lockup waiting to be arraigned. An assistant D.A. named Sophie Spurgeon took them separately into an interview room and walked out shaking her head after each of them told his story. The stories were consistent and accurate except for a couple of minor details, such as the existence of the $100,000 in payoff money and what happened to it. Both Ruffin and McGrath had concluded that if they never mentioned the $100,000, nobody else was going to bring it up. Certainly not Chung or his uncle, who wouldn't want to admit that they had any reason to pay hush money, or the cops, who'd intended to steal it and probably thought one of them had succeeded. Assistant D.A. Spurgeon assured Ruffin that Jayden and Derek were doing fine and that Detective Morales, now a decorated hero, would be back on the job in a few days.

The two parolees were also being hailed as heroes. The media featured them in nonstop coverage of the Commissioner's downfall and the scandal of the dirty cops. Protestors outside City Hall demanded that Ruffin and McGrath be released immediately. The governor invited them to Sacramento to address the legislature about the need for reform. The District Attorney, up for re-election, announced that he wouldn't press charges for anything they had done since their release from San Quentin. McGrath was pumped up, triumphant but still determined to get his money. Ruffin prayed that no witnesses or surveillance videos would surface that might reveal where the money had gone. And he hoped that Derek understood and followed his instructions about the fishing tackle box, even if it meant prying the trunk open with a crowbar.

After two nights in the lockup, half a dozen guards escorted them out of the lockup in their orange jumpsuits. News reporters and camera crews surged around them shouting questions as they were bundled into Chung's Lincoln Town Car, where they rode in the back seat like celebrities. Felipe drove them to Chung's uncle's restaurant for a dim sum feast complete with candlelight, linen napkins and silverware so heavy that McGrath decided not to slip any of it into his orange jumpsuit. Black-tied waiters buzzed in and out with an array of dishes — steamed chicken feet, fried turnip cake, sticky rice — which, to McGrath's taste, didn't seem a whole lot different from prison food. "We sure appreciate this dinner, Mr. Chung," he said. "Even though I got to say the portions are a little small."

"I'll be sure to mention that to my uncle," Chung smiled. "This dinner was all his idea, to show his appreciation for your efforts. You know, he was devastated by what the Commissioner did to that girl."

Ruffin gnawed on his steamed beef tripe and wondered what it was made of. "How did your uncle keep from going down with the Commissioner?" he asked.

"My uncle is like Chuck-E-Cheese," Chung said. "He just provides the venue and the party favors. He's a go-between, a facilitator." Chung poured himself a cup of tea. "But what about you, McGrath? You're the one who brought the girls to the hotel."

"I swear I thought they was going there for shorthand lessons," McGrath said.

"But when you saw the Commissioner there.... "

"That made me wonder, I admit. And when that poor girl was strangled, I knew it must have been that fat bastard that did it. That's why your uncle promised me fifty grand for testifying it was a Russian."

"My uncle's attorney," Chung corrected him.

"What's the difference? He was representing your uncle, wasn't he?"

"Not on that particular matter," Chung said. "The money was to come from third parties. As usual, my uncle was only a go-between. And then you took it on yourself to double the amount you were owed. That was a bad idea that rubbed people the wrong way."

"Anyway, I never got the money," McGrath said. "That satchel you brought to the bank plaza—"

"I know," Chung interrupted, "somebody snatched it when I passed out. But you see, the people who provided that money don't feel they got their money's worth. They're not nice people and they're sticklers about such things."

"I earned that money," McGrath objected.

"Nevertheless, they want it back."

"But I never got it." McGrath thumped the handle of his fork on the table.

"Somehow I think that argument will fall on deaf ears," Chung smiled. "Knowing the kind of people involved."

"I need to talk to your uncle about this," McGrath said.

"My uncle can't help you. Maybe you should talk to the police."

Felipe and a burly bartender stepped up to the table and stood next to Chung with their arms crossed.

"Ain't you the police?" McGrath asked.

Chung shook his head. "Department of Corrections," he smiled. "Completely independent of the police."

McGrath dug into his steamed chicken feet and wondered if he needed to start thinking about an escape plan. "Well, at least we're out of jail, ain't we, Ruffin?" he said. "No problem's too big if you're out of jail."

"I'm not sure you can take much comfort in that," Chung said. "In fact, in view of the people involved and their uncompromising attitude, you might be better off behind bars."

McGrath glanced up warily from his chicken feet. "We ain't in any danger of going back inside, are we?"

Two young men with crewcuts who looked like prison guards appeared at the table and took up positions behind Ruffin and McGrath. They wore khaki chinos, black oxfords, and long-sleeved black shirts. They did not smile.

"I mean," McGrath added, "you can't make an omelet without breaking some eggs, right? You got to look at the big picture."

"When I look at the big picture," Chung said, "you know what I see? Four cops in intensive care, two more in jail — including the Commissioner. A five-million-dollar helicopter in the scrap heap, along with three squad cars. An oil refinery burned to the ground and still smoldering — the experts say it might burn until the end of the world."

Ruffin knew where this was going. McGrath still didn't seem to get it.

"As your parole agent," Chung said, "it's hard to ignore all that."

"The D.A.'s office says they ain't gonna press charges," McGrath pointed out.

"Again, this is Corrections, not the D.A.'s office," Chung said. "We have our own standards."

A second pair of unsmiling crewcuts in long-sleeved black shirts joined the others behind the chairs. Ruffin felt the two behind his chair set their toes against its back legs so he couldn't move. "I was afraid you'd say that," he said.

"You mean you're sending us back inside?" McGrath asked incredulously.

"I can see that in your case," Chung said, sipping his tea, "dim is more than the sum of its parts. To spell it out for you, McGrath: this will be your last fine dining experience for a while. Starting tomorrow, your room and board will be provided by the Department of Corrections in picturesque Marin County."

McGrath tried to negotiate one final point. "Can't we get into one of them country club prisons?" he asked. "You know, that has a golf course?"

"Sorry, Cat," Chung said. "You're going back to San Quentin."

McGrath's eyes darted desperately around the room.

"Look at it this way," Chung said. "I'm giving you another chance. Next time you get out, maybe you won't make the same mistakes."

"Yeah."

"I doubt it, though," Chung smiled.

The two pairs of crewcuts grabbed Ruffin and McGrath from behind, handcuffed them and marched them toward the door.

"By the way," Chung called after them, "the former Commissioner and Detective Burke and some of the others will be joining you up in San Quentin before too long. I hope you and the other prisoners will give them the welcome they deserve."

One week later, at the L.A. County Jail, a contingent of sheriff's deputies escorted Ruffin and McGrath to a Department of Corrections bus for the trip back to San Quentin. Their path out to the bus was blocked by a crowd of well-wishers, including Detective Morales, Shanise, Jayden, Derek, and Grijalva's sister, as well as a few strangers and news reporters.

"Good luck!" someone shouted.

"We'll be waiting for you!"

"Take care of yourself!"

"Peace, brother!"

Morales had one arm in a sling and the other angled over a crutch as she limped along next to Ruffin toward the bus. She'd spent an agonizing few days wrestling with her shock, her pain, her inadequacy, her mistakes, her uncertain future as a cop, and her feelings toward Ruffin. It was too early to tell how permanent her injuries would be. Most people in the department offered their support, sent flowers, looked forward to welcoming her back, but others made no secret of their hostility. She'd shot Burke in the back, that was all they needed to know. She'd made the department look bad. Even the new Commissioner seemed to resent her, though he owed her his job. The union was noncommittal, waiting to see how the political winds blew. It made her sick that Ruffin was going back to San Quentin. The rumor mill had already started grinding out lies about them. And she knew that whatever else happened, she'd never live down being there to see him off. She went anyway.

"Good bye, Kenny," she said, trying to smile

"Good bye, Detective," he said.

"Julie," she corrected him. "I'm only here because of you, so you can call me Julie. Even though I'm a cop."

"Okay, Julie," Ruffin smiled.

"You're making progress."

"We're both still alive," he said. "That's something, ain't it?"

"Sure," she smiled.

"How's the little girl?" he asked. "Luisa Salazar."

"She's out of the hospital. She's going to be all right."

"Good," Ruffin said, squeezing Morales's hand. "You take care now."

"You won't be gone long," Morales said. "I'll be waiting for you."

"That's what I'm afraid of," Ruffin laughed. "Every damn cop in L.A.'s gonna be waiting for me."

He hugged Jayden and Shanise, who had visited him in the jail the day before. They both had a pretty good understanding of what to do with the stuff in that fishing tackle box. Shanise would keep it in a safe place, and eventually it would go to Jayden for his education if he stayed out of trouble. If he hung out with gangs or got crossways with the cops, Ruffin had promised to break out of San Quentin and personally kick his ass. Derek nodded respectfully and Ruffin shook his hand. Shanise wiped away her tears.

"See you all soon," Ruffin said.

Grijalva's sister followed McGrath to the bus. "When are you gonna pay me the money you owe me?" she wanted to know.

"Just as soon as I get out, sweetheart," McGrath said.

"When are we gonna get married?"

"The same day I pay you the money."

"How do I know if you'll ever come back?"

The deputies shoved McGrath into the bus, and with his last ounce of resistance he twisted around and raised his voice for the benefit of the crowd.

"The Cat'll come back," he declared. "The Cat always comes back. And I'm gonna get my money. You can count on that."

They were the only passengers on the bus, but the guard shackled them into adjoining seats as if they really were joined at the hip.

"Why do I got to sit here?" Ruffin asked the guard. He pointed toward the other end of the bus. "Why can't I sit over there?"

"This is a Corrections bus," the guard said. "Strictly economy class. You don't get your choice of seats."

McGrath started talking as soon as they were locked in. "Well, here we are again, Ruffin," he said. "Right back where we started. Prison's gonna seem like a picnic after parole, ain't it?"

Ruffin wanted to cover his ears but he couldn't raise his hands. Instead, telling himself not to listen, he stared out the window for a last glimpse of home. There was the soft fog of L.A., the skyscrapers, the hazy mountains in the distance. The bus cruised away from the jail, entered the freeway and headed north toward San Quentin.

"Them sons of bitches up in Quentin," McGrath droned on, "are gonna take one look at me and start singing, 'The cat came back, we thought he was a goner but the cat came back.' They do the same thing every time, like it's a real clever joke that's just as funny the tenth time you heard it. And I hate to admit it, but you know what, Ruffin? They've got a point. I been in and out a few times, and probably will be again. Like I said when we got down here—"

"McGrath," Ruffin said, "if you don't shut up—"

"You can get out of jail, but you never get out of parole."

THE END

About the Author

Bruce Hartman is the author of eight previous novels. *Perfectly Healthy Man Drops Dead,* his first book, won the Salvo Press Mystery Novel Award and published by Salvo Press in 2008. In 2018 it was republished in a slightly revised form. Bruce Hartman's books have ranged from mysteries (*The Rules of Dreaming, The Muse of Violence, The Philosophical Detective*) to comedies (*A Butterfly in Philadelphia, Potlatch: A Comedy*), techno/political satire (*Big Data Is Watching You!*) and a legal thriller (*The Devil's Chaplain*). A graduate of Wesleyan University and Harvard Law School, he lives with his wife in Philadelphia.

Made in the USA
Middletown, DE
27 May 2019